th
RELUCTANT
MANAGER

JAMES BUDD

the
RELUCTANT
MANAGER

ACACIA
BOOKS

ABOUT THE AUTHOR

BORN IN RUGBY, England, during the Second World War, James Budd studied Arabic at Cambridge. He taught English in government secondary schools in Saudi Arabia from 1965 to 1970. Between 1970 and 1983 he worked in Kuwait Oil Company, the Shell Company of Qatar and the Civil Aviation College in Doha.

In 1984 he moved to Muscat, where he worked for two years as a translator and English teacher at a language institute. He joined the Oman News Agency in 1992, returning to England in 1998.

Since then he has lived beside the River Stour near Manningtree on the Essex-Suffolk border.

In affectionate memory of

Khalid, Julie, Yousuf and Abdul Malik

CONTENTS

PREFACE

S hould I call this book a memoir, a novel or a collection of short stories? It has elements of all three, though the country (Khajal) in which the events take place is fictional. Nevertheless, it contains a lot more fact than fiction, its characters are inspired by real people from my past and most of the episodes it describes are either drawn from my own experiences or based on reports from former colleagues, friends and acquaintances. However, to quote Edward in Chapter 11 ("Khajal Revisited"), I have also "juggled around with the people they happened to and the sequence and locations in which they occurred" and on more than one occasion I have allowed my imagination, such as it is, to add a few extra touches.

Although the state in which this story took place does not exist on any map, some elderly expatriates who remember the Gulf region from some forty years ago might feel that there is an uncanny similarity between Khajal and a certain small emirate about half way down the Arabian side of the Gulf as it was in the mid to late 1970s. If they do, then I should like to say that their suspicions may or may not be correct, but any resemblance to specific, identifiable individuals is unintentional and coincidental.

While I personally can see nothing in this book that could cause offence, several well-meaning "Khajali" friends and acquaintances have warned me that some of their more sensitive fellow-citizens might not appreciate that this is a work of fiction and, if I were to refer to their country by its real name, accuse me of casting aspersions on it and its people and persuade the authorities to put me on their no-entry black list. For me, this would be a great pity because I still try to spend a few days there every year to pick up the threads with old friends.

I am happy to report that my surviving "Khajali" friends from half a century ago continue to be close friends today and, whether we meet in England or "Khajal", we find we are still able to relive our younger days though each other's memories. Sadly, however, in recent years it is becoming increasingly difficult for me to relate the country's present-day physical reality to my recollections of the places I used to enjoy in the 1970s. Those of us who lived there during that time remember it as an endearingly intimate, relaxed and rather ramshackle sort of country, and we would never have dreamt that within a few decades its capital city would be transformed into one of the most modern, frenetic and soullessly efficient metropolises of our 21st century world.

Although most of this book was written between 2022 and 2024, I wrote the first two chapters in 1979. It was during that time that the name "Khajal" (an Arabic word which can mean "diffidence", but also "shame" or "ignominy"), was suggested to me by a "Khajali" friend while he was suffering from a fit of depression about the direction his country was taking in the early years of the oil boom and what he saw as its departure from its traditional way of life.

1.

BETTER LUCK NEXT TIME - PERHAPS

It was a hot, humid afternoon in October 1975. The day's work was over. The siren had sounded and cars were streaming from offices and workshops towards Mottled Oil's exit gate.

The car park outside the Main Office was still full. It also had its daily ritual, but it was not regulated by the siren. In a few minutes, some fifty pairs of eyes would take up their positions behind the venetian blinds and fix their gaze on the Managing Director's Mercedes. Its departure would be the signal for his underlings to put away their files, cover their typewriters and pack their handbags and briefcases. Only then would they feel free to drive home with their reputations for diligence still intact.

Most of the Personnel Department staff had already arrived at the Company's nearby Social Centre and were seated on plush green thrones round the walls of the fiercely air-conditioned Small Party Room.

They were a mixture of nationalities. Daffodil de Souza, Myrtle Lobo, Lavender Sequeira and Marie-Antoinette Williams were typists from Bombay; Mahmoud Omar, Samir Touqan and

Walid al Qasim were Palestinian; Steve Kettle, Roy Sladen, Peter Frazer, Mike Kelly and the guest of honour were English. The only Khajalis present were Mubarak al Mansuri and Migbil al Ameri.

Apart from Mubarak and Migbil, nearly all of them had been with the Company for years. They knew each other well and in normal circumstances relations between them - both in and out of work - were generally casual and relaxed.

This, however, was a Personnel Department Farewell-to-One-of-Our Colleagues Tea Party - an event that was really an extension of work, though everyone had to pretend it was an informal get-together. As usual on such occasions, the dilemma of "Are we still officially colleagues or are we supposed to be meeting as friends?" had put a strain on the gathering. There were smiles aplenty, it is true, though they were a little forced and conversation was nervous and stilted. The guest of honour - a thin, lank-haired, tense-looking main in his late twenties - examined his shirt-cuffs, looked at the curtains and glanced from time to time at the purple carpet with its exuberant pattern of golden wreaths.

The hydraulic double doors opened with a discreet sigh and a hush fell upon the room. An Indian in a starched linen jacket brought in a white cloth and headed for the trestle table by the window. Another followed, pushing a trolley laden with sandwiches, samosas, cold sausage rolls, cheese straws, rock buns and little cakes topped with green and pink icing. A third bore a tray of cups, jugs of milk and bowls of sugar, and a fourth had a large pot of tea in one hand and an asbestos mat in the other.

The cloth was spread and the table was laid. Two of the waiters wheeled the trolley out. The other two stood by stiffly.

A cockroach scuttled across the floor, but no-one interfered with its progress. When it reached the wall it climbed up one of the curtains and settled on top of the pelmet, its antennae waving.

Mubarak was looking out of the window.

"The big boss is going," he announced.

The Personnel Manager would arrive soon. A few stomachs started to churn at the prospect of the snacks they were about to receive.

Conversation revived.

"So how are you?" Mubarak asked Migbil for a third time, to ensure that he had heard the answer correctly.

"May Allah be praised," replied Migbil. "What's your news?"

"Good, may your life be long," said Mubarak. "How is your health?"

"It's fine - may Allah keep you safe," said Migbil.

The typists discussed ways of preparing shepherd's pie, prawn masala, chicken pulao, Yorkshire pudding and other delicacies from home and the pages of "*Woman's Own*".

The rest engaged in desultory small talk about how they spent their spare time and what they felt about living in Khajal.

Footsteps approached and a high-pitched giggle wafted through the door.

"Ah, Kamal," Migbil muttered darkly. "I'd recognize that spiteful titter anywhere."

George Weever, the Personnel Manager, came in and beamed at the company. He was a large-boned, bluff man in his mid-fifties, grey-haired and balding, with little eyes set above pouches which were several sizes too big for them. His nose was slightly tinged with purple, though he had a healthy, ruddy complexion.

His two assistants were delayed for a few moments by an "after you" battle at the door. This was resolved by Kamal, who followed his boss.

Kamal's appointment as the Company's Head of Human Resources Development was generally seen as an ingenious Mottled Oil plot to keep qualified Khajalis as far away as possible from the levers of power. He was a Palestinian, hence regarded by the British top brass as "expendable when expedient" (in a former Managing Director's immortal words), and he saw Khajalis as posing a danger to his own job security.

His solution to this threat was to tell the expatriate management repeatedly - as an Arab who understood "these people" and had his finger on the native pulse - that the locals had no potential.

As he was in charge of recruitment too, he found it easy to deal with the stray Khajali applicant who showed signs of exceptional intelligence and drive.

"Too ambitious," he would write in the comments section of the application form. "This man expects to get to the top in the shortest possible time. His test results show that he is quite bright, but such a person would be a disruptive influence. Not recommended."

Hussain Abbas al Marri was the last to enter. As Personnel Affairs Supervisor, he was the top Khajali in the Company. He had been with Mottled for nearly twenty years, rising slowly from tea-boy to trainee clerk to clerk. He had halted at that position for some time, but his zeal in reporting the misdemeanours of his fellow employees came to the notice of the higher-ups and he was made a trainee Personnel Officer.

Here he also had the chance to show that the Company's interests were very much his own and, being in daily contact with the senior management, he was able to mould himself gradually into a passable imitation of the "good Mottled type".

He had been in his present post for two years - a credit to Mottled and a tangible answer to those critics in the Khajali government who accused the Company of dragging its feet over Khajalisation.

"See, we've got a Cadgerly in a top job," Mottled's English Managing Director had said to the Minister of Petroleum on Hussain's promotion. "Don't worry, Your Excellency. We are pushing your people forward and the proof of the pudding is in the eating, I always say."

"True," said the Minister after a short pause while he struggled to see how pudding could be relevant in that context. "But Hussain's not really one of us, you know. He's actually an Iranian. Al Marri are a Bedouin Arab tribe and no genuine Marri has a name like Hussain or Abbas. Of course, he has Khajali nationality, wears Khajali dress and speaks Arabic just like we do, but he doesn't fool any of us."

"Sorry we're late," said George Weever, sitting down on a vacant throne beside the guest of honour. "Few things to tie up at the office. Fatty couldn't make it, I'm afraid. Had to go down to the Marine Department." Fathi, a Palestinian, was Weever's trouble-shooter - a bull-like man with an intimidating roar who was hated and feared by the daily-paid labourers.

Tea was served and the typists brought round the plates of food.

"Where is it you're off to, Edward?" Weever asked the guest of honour. "Beirut isn't it?"

"Yes," said Edward.

"Lovely city," said Weever. "Or so I hear. Never been there myself. Dorothy and I always go back to the UK for our hols. Looking forward to it?"

"Yes," said Edward. "Though I'll miss Khajal."

"Of course," Weever agreed. "Lovely place, Cadgel... Mubarak!" he called across the room, "I was just saying to Edward what a lovely place Cadgel is."

Mubarak smiled.

"Of course," he said. "Khajal is the best lovely place."

At the next lull Weever rose to his feet.

"Well, we all know why we're here," he announced. "But first, as is my usual custom, absent friends.

"We've had news of quite a lot of old Mottledites recently... Michael and Jane Weston have settled down well in their cottage near Torquay and you probably won't be surprised to hear that Michael is putting in plenty of time at the local golf club. Jane, as usual, is doing wonders with their garden.

"Phil and Brenda Newt. Golly, it must be all of three years since they left! How time flies! Some of you might not remember them. Phil used to be in charge of Finance...

"Where was I? Oh, yes. Phil and Brenda send regards to you all from Winchester. Sorry, Chichester... Lovely county, Sussex. Phil's doing great things in the Conservative Club over there and Brenda says he's really got their bar properly sorted out. And they see quite a lot of Reg and Maureen Badcock.

"John and Paula Pratt." He looked grave. "Some sad news I'm afraid. I expect one or two of you may have heard it already. You know John had that liver trouble for years. Well, he passed away during last year's festive season. Terrible blow for Paula, but she says in her latest letter that John didn't suffer at all and he continued to enjoy life right up to the very end. Over Christmas he was the life and soul of all the parties; then he suddenly collapsed just before the New Year."

He paused and glanced at a scrap of paper in his hand before putting on a confiding smile.

"Before we really get down to business, I'd just like to say a few words about what we've been up to in our department recently.

"As you know, Mottled is doing its bit to help Cadgerlies move up the ladder. For example, Hussain here."

Hussain al Marri smiled faintly and inclined his head in acknowledgement.

"And others. Migbil was promoted to filing clerk only a few weeks ago and he is doing a jolly good job. And Mubarak should be getting promoted soon." He winked at Mubarak.

"That's only in Personnel. But throughout the Company, Cadgerlies with potential are being prepared for higher things and they will be moved up when the time is ripe. I can say that Mottled has every reason to be proud of itself in this respect."

Fearing for their own career prospects, some of the non-Khajali employees looked faintly anxious, but they smiled nonetheless.

Weever turned to Edward.

"Edward Holdsworth has been with us for... what, three years is it Edward?"

"Four," said Edward.

"Four years. Quite a long time. Edward of course is on contract to us from the Monotone School and he and his chums have been doing a splendid job at the Training Centre, teaching English to our Cadgerly employees... Normally we don't put on shows like this afternoon's for contract staff, but Edward and Monotone are such good chaps that we think of them as honorary Mottledites. And as Edward is the longest-serving Monotone teacher since our relationship began, we in Personnel felt we should do something to show our appreciation for his services.

"Edward is off to Beirut next week to join Monotone over there and I'm sure you will all join with me in wishing him all the very best."

The company clapped politely.

"So we would like to ask Edward to accept this small present - have you got it Camel?" Kamal handed him a package. "Thank you... this small present as a token of our esteem and thanks."

He held it in Edward's direction. Edward went up to him, shook his free hand and accepted the gift.

Everyone clapped.

Then Edward went through Phase One of the Mottled Procedure for Recipients of Farewell Gifts from Their Departments. This consisted of unwrapping the package, discovering to his delight that it contained a gold-plated pen and pencil set, presenting it to the occupant of the nearest throne so that it could be passed round and admired, and smiling vaguely into space until everyone had examined it and expressed approval.

Phase Two was the Leaver's Speech.

"Thank you all very much indeed," said Edward. "Thank you for your generosity in giving me this beautiful present and thank you, er, George, for honouring me by considering me an honorary Mottledite, for which I am - erm - truly honoured."

He paused. That sentence had seemed quite elegant when he was preparing to trip it off his tongue but, having tripped it off, he felt it sounded rather clumsy.

He continued.

"I've enjoyed working for Mottled and the years I've spent in Khajal have been among the happiest of my life. I'm going to miss this place. I'm going to miss the job, but most of all I'm going to miss you - all of you and..."

"And we're going to miss you too Edward," Weever interrupted cheerfully.

"Thank you, er, George... As I was saying... I'm going to miss you all, and Khajal, and the job... but I'm looking forward to Beirut too, of course. I'm going to be the Assistant Director of Studies in their school there, which will be a step up for me. And Lebanon is a lovely country. I've been there quite a few times and I love it."

The sound of a *sotto voce* raspberry emanated quietly but unmistakeably from the general direction of where his English colleagues were sitting and some of the audience suppressed a temptation to snigger.

"As you probably know," Edward continued, looking slightly flustered, "there's been a bit of trouble there recently - gun battles and that sort of thing. But I rang the Lebanese Embassy this morning and they told me everything was fine and not to worry.

Apparently the whole business was just a little sectarian problem and it's all been sorted out now.

"Anyway, thank you all very much again. We must keep in touch. If any of you come to Beirut, please give me a ring. You can contact me through the Monotone School there. Thank you."

The gentle applause signalled the start of the Final Phase.

Weever went and stood by the door. Edward joined him. The others formed an orderly queue, waiters at the rear, shook hands with their departing colleague and left.

The waiters began to clear away the cups and plates. Weever took Edward's hand and gave it an intimate squeeze.

"Look after yourself old chap," he said. "All the best and don't forget to keep in touch."

One of the waiters dropped a cup and saucer. Weever's little eyes suddenly blazed with anger.

"Watch what you're doing, you bloody idiot," he barked.

He was a man who liked to ration his affability and he preferred not to squander it on the servant class.

*　*　*　*

"You really are a bit of a creep, you know," said Peter Frazer as they drove back into town. (He was Edward's housemate – a tall, skinny young man in his early twenties with a mop of untidy fair hair.) "You had a perfect chance to tell them what you thought of them and all you did was beam at everybody like a... like a..."

"Cheshire cat?"

"Exactly. Couldn't have put it better myself. Grin like a Cheshire cat and say how much you loved them all. That raspberry was fair comment."

"Well, you would say that. It was you who did it, wasn't it? None of the others would have had the gall... They'd have had a bit more respect for my feelings. And as for you... you know I'm terrified of speaking in public. You saw the state I was in before the party."

"OK. Yes, it was me. I admit it and I apologise."

"Accepted... Though I noticed that you were pretty creepy yourself most of the time... Your simpering smile when you were talking to Hussain al Marri... and you seemed to be hanging on every word of the speeches... even mine, until you thought it would be amusing to put me off my stride."

"But you're leaving so you've got nothing to lose. I have to crawl a bit because I have to stay here. For the time being, anyway."

"Look," said Edward, "I don't..."

A car whizzed past on the inside lane and shot across in front of them. Peter hooted a long, petulant blast. The passengers turned round and waved to him. He blushed and waved back.

"Those bloody trainees! That's the second time they've cut me up this week!" he exclaimed. "Why are they still hanging around at this end of the town anyway?"

"Well, one of them told me this morning he'd managed to get hold of a bottle of Scotch for a hundred and fifty riyals so I suspect they've probably been down to the jetty for a few quick ones," Edward said. "As you know, they often go there for an after-work tipple on the sly."

"Honestly, the black market prices they charge these days! He must have been desperate to pay that much ... Anyway, I still say it was a pretty creepy performance on your part. You're always going on about how racist the management is and how they pretend to be pro-Khajali when the last thing they want is a Khajali in a really high position. And now you've suddenly started telling them how much you're going to miss them all. Perhaps you've got converted to Mottledism in your old age?"

"Of course not. Don't be ridiculous," Edward said. "But there's no point in making enemies just for the sake of it. If I'd insulted them, George Weever would probably have sent a nasty letter about me to Monotone and if he'd been seriously outraged he might even have threatened not to renew our contract with them. That wouldn't do me or anyone else any good. I want this to be the year I escape from Monotone, not the year I join the dole queue."

*   *   *   *

Nicky Wood, the local Monotone branch manager, came round to their flat that evening.

"Oh, Edward," he said. "I had a message from Beirut this afternoon."

"Great." Edward smiled in pleasurable anticipation. "Are they getting ready to roll out the red carpet for me?"

"Well, that's what I wanted to talk to you about." Nicky looked shifty. "Bad news I'm afraid. Apparently all hell's broken out over there."

"What do you mean?! What's happened?"

"Beirut seems to have sort of erupted. The school had two direct shell hits today and was more or less demolished. Fortunately it happened just before dawn so it was closed and nobody was inside."

The colour drained from Edward's face.

"Please tell me you're joking," he said.

"If only I were."

"God, what a disaster! So that's the end of my job then. And Monotone Lebanon."

"I'm afraid it looks like it," agreed Nicky. "But... on a brighter note, if it's any consolation to you, you're not going to be stuck with nowhere to go. I rang Weever earlier this evening and told him what had happened and he was very sympathetic. Now he's just called me back to say that Mottled are prepared to offer you a six-month special assignment with them, so if you want it you are safely employed till the end of March next year."

"I suppose I should be grateful... Well, I am grateful, but I had set my sights so much on escaping from Mottled Oil and... well, what can I say?" Edward groaned.

"It's probably a blessing in disguise," Nicky said. "If not, you can just put it down to fate. You and Mottled are clearly destined to be stuck with each other for a little longer."

2.

INTERLUDE

The invitation had been extended and accepted.

"OK, so that's it then," said Salim, the star of Tech 2a (Edward's former class) as the trainees prepared to leave Mottled Oil's Training Centre at the start of the weekend. "We'll pick you up at four o'clock on Thursday... that's, tomorrow afternoon. Don't forget." (Khajal's weekend was Thursday and Friday.)

"But are you absolutely sure you don't want me to bring anything?" Edward said. "I really feel I ought to contribute."

"No," Salim insisted. "Just yourself and whatever you need for sleeping. We have arranged all the food and Ahmed is bringing his tent."

"Well, let me pay for my share of the food."

"No." There was a chorus of protests.

"All right then," said Edward. "If you insist."

The technical trainees looked expectantly at Abdulaziz - the oldest and least reticent member of the group. There was a pause.

"If you really think you would like to bring something, perhaps you could help us a little," he said. "But I'm afraid this may be a trouble for you."

"No, no. I'll help in any way I can," Edward said. "Just tell me what it is you want."

"We have been looking for something to drink because, as they say, 'A camping trip without drink has no flavour.' We have not succeeded in finding any yet. If you could bring a little... No... Maybe you could just be ready to bring some in case we can't get any. We are still asking our friends and I am sure we shall be successful."

Khajal was a semi-dry country. Non-Muslims on a certain salary level could get liquor-permits which entitled them to a monthly drink allowance. Muslims were forbidden access to alcohol.

"No. No. No. Let me handle the drink," said Edward. "I'll bring a bottle of Scotch."

"That's very kind of you," said Abdulaziz. "Truly. But you shouldn't bother... Still, if it's really no trouble to you, maybe you could manage two bottles... Just a minute, there are eight of us. Would three bottles be all right?"

"Ahmed and I only drink beer," said Sa'd, a fat youth just out of his teens with a gentle face and a wisp of beard.

"Sorry, Edward. I'd forgotten about them. What would really be fantastic if you could do it would be three... no, let's say two bottles of whisky and a case of beer. Is that OK?"

This amounted to nearly half Edward's monthly drink allowance. He gulped and did a quick calculation.

"Yes," he said with a weak smile. "I'll bring two bottles of Scotch and a case of beer. No problem at all."

The trainees broke into smiles of relief, approval and gratitude.

"*Wallahi*, Edward. You are a very good man," said Abdulaziz. "That is more than enough. You really shouldn't trouble yourself... Oh... We shall be out for two nights - Thursday and Friday - won't we? No, that's all right. If we ration our drinking carefully on

Thursday night, I'm sure we'll have no problem... Though perhaps, just to make sure, you could bring three bottles of whisky."

"Isn't it rather a waste of a weekend if we spend all the time drinking and having hangovers?" Edward said.

"Yes, you are right," Abdulaziz agreed. "Two bottles would be fine. And the beer of course. We'll collect you tomorrow afternoon. Make sure you are ready as we must be on the road by four at the latest."

"OK, but just as a matter of interest, where is it we're heading for?" Edward asked. "Or haven't you decided yet?"

"Yes, we've decided for sure but not one hundred per cent," Salim replied. "Anyway, we're going to a nice place."

*　　*　　*　　*

It was November 1975. About a month had gone by since Edward's farewell-tea-party-that-wasn't and during the past four weeks he had been trying to justify his presence on his "six-month special assignment" with Mottled Oil.

Monotone had not been asked to send out a replacement for him because Mottled had decided to cut back on its English courses and reduce the number of English teachers from five to four. This meant that Edward had been timetabled out of the training programme, so consequently Mottled were at a loss to know quite what to do with him.

At first they suggested he might try to put the Training Centre's filing system into some sort of logical order, but he found it so chaotic, incomprehensible and utterly devoid of rhyme or reason that, after two days of gnashing his teeth and tearing out his hair, he gave up in despair.

Next, George Weever thought it might be a good idea if he could help devise a more effective system for liaising between the Training Centre and the other departments, but this was vetoed by the Managing Director on the grounds that a task of that magnitude required a Mottled Oil senior staff member and Edward was not actually a Company employee.

Finally, it was Edward himself who proposed a solution.

"What about a new Mottled Oil English course with more appropriate vocabulary?" he suggested. "The technical teachers are always complaining that our standard Janet and John courses aren't relevant, with their stories about... you know... things like trips to the cinema and helping mother in the kitchen... so perhaps I could try to produce something a bit closer to what they want."

"Good idea," Weever said.

So Edward was given an office of his own and the management arranged a programme of field visits so that he could see the young Khajali mechanics, tugmen and drilling rig workers at work after they had finished their technical training. Although he was no longer teaching, he was still based at the Training Centre, so he kept in close touch with his old class and he was delighted when they invited him to join them on a weekend in the desert.

*　　*　　*　　*

Shortly after five o'clock on the day of the trip - around an hour later than originally planned - Salim's battered minibus collected Edward from his house and it was now heading through Khajal City's eastern fringes with the rest of the group on board.

They passed several huge half-completed housing estates - high-walled compounds of stark little villas, many still without roofs, separated from each other by rubbly dirt tracks. By the roadside, large hoardings in Arabic and English proclaimed:

"Fifty houses for the people of Khajal. Yousuf bin Khalid Contracting Co." "Manfred Limpet. Pipes and Manholes" "Twenty houses for the people of Khajal. H. A. Al Marri, Builders and Contractors", "Eighty Houses for the people of Khajal. Project of H.H. the Emir. Execution by LBW Contractors" "Al Ahmed-Scraggins for earth-moving equipment"...

Scattered beside the road were bulldozers, piles of rubble and hunks of broken concrete exuding twisted metal rods.

"The new Welfare Housing Project," Ahmed explained. He was a small, bird-like young man with a friendly innocent face.

The road suddenly narrowed and its surface became pitted and bumpy. Khajal City slipped behind them and they were in the desert.

The terrain was typical of central and western Khajal - fine, hard-packed dust, yellow-grey, strewn with stones and small boulders, so flat that the horizon showed the curve of the earth's surface and thinly sprinkled with a covering of dark green and crimson succulent plants, scrawny tufts of coarse, greenish-yellow grass and occasional thorny acacia bushes. They passed a few of the ruling family's out-of-town palaces - isolated buildings with sloping roofs tiled green or pink, their upper-story verandas half screened by garishly-painted colonnades, and the tops of eucalyptus, tamarisk and flame-trees peering over their garden walls.

A row of oil pipelines snaked up, ran alongside them for a few miles and zig-zagged gradually away again as the road swung southwards.

* * * *

"Ouf! It's half past five!" Salim exclaimed, pulling his sleeve down over his watch. "It's all your fault Ahmed, may Allah destroy your house. We'll never get there before sunset."

"Look, may Allah forgive you, I've already said sorry twice," Ahmed replied heatedly. "What more do you want me to do? Kiss your shoes? Or some other part of your anatomy? And anyway, as I told you, it wasn't my fault I was late... If mothers want you to take them out visiting, you can hardly say no, can you? ... I begged my mother to make it short but the people we went to see wouldn't let us leave."

"All right, all right. Don't get upset," said Salim. "We spent an hour waiting for you but it was OK really..."

"OK if you like hanging around in other people's houses when you want to be on the road..." one of the others interrupted.

"...and your little brother was very generous with the coffee and dates," Salim continued. "It's just that we're going to have a problem putting up the tent as there's no moon tonight."

"Let me worry about that," said Ahmed, mollified. "It's my tent and I've put it up hundreds of times. We'll have it up in five minutes."

*   *   *   *

"Our turning is coming up now," Abdulaziz said, pointing to a dark shape a few hundred yards ahead of them.

They reached it and stopped. On the right side of the road was a sun-bleached camel's skull on a rusty oil-drum. The tarmac just beyond it was smudged with dust where a track led off into the wilderness.

They drove over the rough ground. After a hundred yards or so the track became two, then three, then four, each strand criss-crossing and looping over the others like the imprint of a gigantic loose plait.

The tracks had been worn down by years of use, but the minibus had to crawl cautiously to avoid plunging into the dried-up rivulets that crossed their path from time to time and were all but invisible until they were almost on top of them.

Three or four miles off the main road, the ground rose slightly in front of them. When they reached the top of the rise they could see a bowl below them several hundred yards across. Two tall date palms stood at one end of it; the rest was sparsely thicketed with thorn-bushes and dwarf tamarisks and a wave of barren ground rose gently on the far side. A few sheep and camels were browsing among the greenery.

"There must be a Bedu camp nearby," Salim said. "Never mind. There are other places not far from here that are just as good."

At the edge of the bowl the tracks became more decisive; two swung sharply to the left, the other two to the right.

"Left here," said Ahmed.

"No, right," said Hassan firmly, and uncharacteristically. The quietest and least assertive member of the group, he was the quintessential yes-man and rarely expressed a contrary opinion on any subject.

"What do you think, Obeid?" Salim asked. "You've been here before, haven't you?"

Obeid had been to many places before, but the outside world failed to register with him unless it involved football, girls or food.

"*Wallah*i... left," he said. "Or maybe right. I can't remember exactly."

"None of you have a clue," Abdulaziz said. "We must go left."

"Eat your own shit, the lot of you," Salim said casually. "We'll go left. If we get stuck it won't be my fault."

They skirted the edge of the bowl. A herdsman standing by a bush stared at them and scowled. A kink in the track took them into a grazing area and past a large, dark brown hair tent; an open space in front of it was occupied by a couple of pick-up trucks decorated with painted wrought-ironmongery. Three young women fled as they approached, brightly coloured chinks of silk and nylon flashing from beneath the hems of their black cloaks.

A Bangladeshi was sitting on an orange crate in front of the tent peeling potatoes.

"The Hour is near," Sa'd intoned. "When the Bedu become rich and have foreigners working for them, that is among the Signs of the Day of Judgement."

"I take refuge in Allah from Satan," exclaimed Ahmed, shocked by Sa'd's flippant impiety. "The Prophet never said anything of the kind, peace be upon him. He spoke of many Signs, like 'When iron speaks' and 'When distant things become near' - that is to say, telephones, and radio and television - but he never said anything about the Bedu having Bangladeshi servants."

Over the next rise was another bowl, thinly wooded with scrub and without palm trees. As they descended towards it a *dhobb* - a spiny-tailed lizard - more than two feet long blundered across in front of them and disappeared into a burrow.

"It's past his bed-time," said Saleh, a swarthy bearded man with a hard face and piercing eyes, who was considered to be an expert on desert lore. "He must have a problem. A snake or something."

"Or a scorpion in his bedroom," Sa'd suggested.

"Of course he has a scorpion in his bedroom!" said Saleh witheringly. "All *dhobb*s share their houses with scorpions. Everybody knows that!"

*   *   *   *

They stopped at a clearing in the midst of the bushes. Cinders and a cluster of fire-blackened stones, some empty tomato puree tins and a tattered Al-Sad Sopermarket plastic carrier-bag dangling from an acacia twig showed that this was a tried and tested camping spot. The sun had just set. The western sky was fading from lemon to grey and the little silvery-pink clouds above the horizon were darkening.

"Tent first," Ahmed said. "Everything else can wait."

*   *   *   *

It was about eight o'clock and, considering that it was late November, it was a surprisingly warm evening. The tent had been pitched, with some difficulty. A cauldron of chickens was stewing over a brushwood fire. A hurricane lamp on a nearby rock cast a small yellow circle of light; the tent and the nearest bushes were just visible beyond its outer periphery as ghostly forms merging with their own and each other's shadows. The burning wood hissed and crackled, throwing out sparks and little embers, while the cauldron-lid trembled resonantly, emitting puffs of steam, which rose from it and mingled with the smoke from the fire.

Obeid was looking after the food. Ahmed and Sa'd were somewhere out of sight; they had wandered off a while ago, cans of Heineken in hand, to forage for more wood. The rest were sitting by the fire drinking whisky and water.

Do you ever have sky like this in England?" Salim asked.

"I don't think so," said Edward.

"Just look at it!" said Salim in an awed voice. "*Ya salam*! Isn't it beautiful! All those millions of stars. How can people think there is no God? And every star is in its right place, doing its appointed duty. Look at those patterns - *al Jabbar, al Dubb al Akbar, al Thurayya* - and those swirls of milky light! How could anyone be so blind as to say that the universe has no Creator? What do you say, Edward?"

"*I*'ve never said that there is no God," Edward replied, "but there is no proof that a God exists."

Hassan took a large gulp of whisky and sighed.

"Edward, I feel you are like my brother," he said, his eyes filling with sentimental tears. "Like my brother, but you are blind. A man may study until he gets three doctorates, but if he doubts the existence of the Creator he is as ignorant as a little child."

Obeid was busy examining the chickens and prodding them

with a spare tent-peg, but the others voiced their approval of Hassan's remarks, commenting that it must have been the whisky that moved him to actually say what he thought for a change.

Ahmed approached, dragging a dead bush; he was limping and had a martyred expression on his face. Sa'd followed, carrying a bouquet of twigs.

"We sat down to finish our beer and Ahmed cut himself on a broken bottle," he explained.

The others laughed.

"You ought to try sitting on a broken bottle," said Ahmed indignantly. "Al right, I'm not bleeding much, but I feel as if I've been stabbed to the marrow."

"Well, if it got you on the bone, at least it left your virginity intact," remarked Abdulaziz. "...*Khashmak*, by the way," he added, looking pointedly at Hassan.

Embarrassed, Hassan pulled his thobe down so that it covered his ankles as well as his knees.

"*Khashmak?* Your nose? Why did you say that?" Edward looked puzzled.

"Yes. Your nose. Or sometimes we say 'Shut the shop' - that's to say, 'You're putting all your goods on display'," Salim explained. "It's a polite way of telling a person he's showing bits of himself that he shouldn't."

Dinner was ready. Obeid and Salim unloaded the chickens onto a large enamel platter. Ahmed dragged a sack over from the tent and unpacked a polythene bag of flat loaves and a lace-frilled plastic table cloth with a floral design, which he spread on the ground and weighted with a little pile of loaves at each corner. Obeid brought the platter over.

*　　*　　*　　*

They squatted to eat, all except Hassan who was reclining against a roll of bedding with his eyes three-quarters closed and a blissful smile on his face.

The whisky was finished and they had all switched to beer. There was a slight breeze and the bushes were sighing in the background.

"Edward, the head of your country... what's her name... Izilibith... she is a woman. Why is that?" Abdulaziz asked.

"I know why," said Obeid. "I read about it the other day. England always has queens, not kings. Nobody knows why but their royal family never gives birth to boys. Only girls."

"You're thinking of Holland," said Edward.

"I know why your ruler is a woman," Saleh interrupted. "It's because there aren't any men in England. If the English were real men they wouldn't allow themselves to be ruled by a woman. That's the reason... For sure, *Wallahi.*"

Hassan snorted in his sleep and rolled over.

"Rubbish," said Edward indignantly.

"Well, look at yourself," Abdulaziz said. "You're a good man, but you haven't got much... much... what was that English word Mr. Roy gave us the other day?"

"Oh yes. I remember," Sa'd said. "'Marbles'. Is that the word you mean?"

"No...'wet'... that's it," said Abdulaziz. "'Wet'. You haven't got much 'wet'. Please don't be offended. I'm not saying this is bad."

"I'm not offended," said Edward huffily, "but it's not a nice thing to say to anybody."

"No Azouz," Ahmed interrupted. "Mr. Roy said 'He's wet,' not 'He hasn't got wet'... he wasn't speaking about Edward, of course. And Edward isn't 'wet'. He has lots of personality... more than we have... Don't listen to him, Edward. He's talking rubbish because he's drunk."

"You should be ashamed, Azouz," Salim said. "Edward may be a foreigner, but he's our brother and our friend."

"Salim is right," said Saleh. "It is an Arab's duty to be polite to a foreigner, especially if he is a guest."

Abdulaziz looked sheepish.

"Edward, I'm sorry. What I said just now was quite untrue." He held out his hand. Edward accepted it, then sat staring at the beetles that clambered round the base of the hurricane lamp.

"I'm a bit tired," he said. "See you later."

He withdrew to the tent, unrolled his bedding and, ignoring a visiting gerbil, lay down and slept.

* * * *

"Did you really have to invite him, Salim?" Saleh asked. "I know there's nothing wrong with him, but his blood's a bit heavy and he doesn't understand our customs."

"His blood's heavy? That's not fair. He's no more boring than most Khajalis I know," Salim replied. "In fact, I enjoy his company. And in any case, he's an old friend of ours and we don't get a chance to see much of him now that he's working on that special assignment."

"It's bad to talk about other people behind their backs," said Ahmed, leaning forward and looking at Saleh accusingly. "We're already committing one sin tonight with the drink, and so far Allah has seen fit not to punish us. If we add malicious gossip to our crimes He may decide to teach us a lesson."

Hassan let out a long breath through shuddering lips.

"Empty words," he mumbled, shifting his position. His head slipped off the bedding and landed on the ground with a thud. He slept on.

"Well, what I say is, you've got to take the thorn with the rose," said Abdulaziz, ignoring Ahmed's and Hassan's observations. "I don't generally care for English people, though Edward's all right. The trouble is, we can't relax when he's around. As Saleh says, he doesn't really understand us, so we have to be over-formal with him all the time."

He took a sip from his can of beer.

"On the other hand, he is useful. He knows the Mottled management, so he can put in a good word for us when we need it... and of course he can get us drink sometimes..."

By Allah, that's a bit cold-blooded," said Salim. "Friends should be friends and no more than that. That's what I believe and that's what I shall always believe."

"That's the way I feel too," Sa'd said, looking serious. "And I think people should always be frank and natural with each other. *I* always behave the same whoever I'm with."

"And that's why everyone thinks you are such a fool," said Abdulaziz. "When you are a little older you'll understand that a man must preserve his dignity. Or at least he should do. Otherwise nobody will respect him."

*   *   *   *

Breakfast the next morning was not a lively affair, though Hassan and Edward had been refreshed by a full night's sleep and were quite bright-eyed. Sa'd had so far resisted all attempts to rouse him; the others sat around, grey and morose, eyes like poached eggs, slurping glasses of tea and nibbling dejectedly at the standard Khajali camping-trip breakfast - flatbread, tinned lemon and melon jam and triangles of plastic cheese.

"What a lovely day!" Edward said, smiling maliciously at Abdulaziz. "What I'd really like is a couple of fried eggs swimming in oil. What would you say to that?" The looks the others gave him were baleful.

An hour or so later the atmosphere had brightened. Sa'd was still asleep, but Salim and Abdulaziz were making plans for the rest of the weekend.

"The beach," Salim said. "That's where I think we should have gone in the first place."

Ahmed agreed and added that he was sure Sa'd would share his opinion. Abdulaziz, who said he was quite happy where he was and saw no reason to move, was strongly backed by Saleh and, less emphatically, Obeid. Edward and Hassan were silent. Eventually, a compromise was reached. The anti-beach group would stay behind and prepare lunch. The rest, who included Edward but not Hassan, would leave as soon as Sa'd and Ahmed were ready and return in the afternoon.

*   *   *   *

Khajal was a small peninsula on the edge of Arabia and nowhere was very far from anywhere else. To travel coast to coast from east to west usually involved a drive of about an hour and a half, and from the northern tip of the country to its south-western border rarely took more than two and a half hours unless there had been heavy rain and the roads were flooded.

It took them a little under an hour to get to the beach from their camp-site; back-tracking towards Khajal City for a few miles and then turning south-east. The sand-dune belt began shortly before they reached the coast. This was a series of yellow, crescent-shaped dunes ranging from fifty to two hundred feet in height, spaced several hundred yards apart from each other, each rising from its own patch of rocky rubble-strewn ground. They had migrated there from the sandy deserts far to the south and west and were still on the move; some of them had wandered onto the road in places, forcing the traffic to make detours onto the rough. Edward felt that a joke would be appropriate.

"If this was England there would be a warning sign saying 'Caution. Dunes crossing'" he said.

The others were impressed by this example of British organisation and Ahmed vowed to write a letter to the Traffic Department.

*   *   *   *

The beach was a wide sandy bay that curved between two large dunes. It was deserted, but although the initial impression to a casual observer was of an idyllic pristine wilderness, from close up the reality was somewhat different; mingled with the seaweed and orange, pink and white shells along the high-water mark was the detritus of generations of passing tankers and freighters - rusting Japanese beer cans, oil clots, planks, broken glass, rotting sacks and scraps of cardboard, metal and plastic.

Ahmed, Sa'd and Edward unloaded the drinking water and the ice-box of soft drinks. Salim followed a little later, looking pleased with himself and carrying a plastic bag that clanked.

They swam. The sea was fresh but comfortable and the sun was hot. Then they sat on the sand and played cards.

Ahmed felt thirsty and opened the ice-box.

"Wouldn't you like something stronger than Kola?" Salim asked with a mysterious look on his face.

"Yes. I'm just in the mood for it," Ahmed replied, "but we finished the beer last night."

Salim took a bottle of what looked like chalky water out of his bag.

"Emergency supplies," he explained. "I was afraid we might get through Edward's drink too quickly, so I brought a couple of bottles of local stuff. Don't worry. It's locally distilled, but it's clean."

"I only drink beer," said Ahmed, shaking his head.

"But if you mix it with Kola or lemonade, you'll get a nice feeling from it and you'll hardly taste anything at all," said Salim.

"Oh, what the hell!" said Ahmed after a few moments. "I'll give it a go."

"Good man... What about you, Sa'd?"

"No, no. I've tried that stuff before and it made me sick. As we haven't got any beer, I'll stick to Kola."

* * * *

They started back just before three. When they were a few miles from their camp-site, Salim suddenly felt inspired to practice his desert driving.

"Weaving always feels better than going straight," he giggled, winding across the road from right to left, left to right. "Oops. Hit a rock there I think. They ought to make roads that wriggle so that drivers can handle them more easily."

Sa 'd, who had stuck to the soft drinks, was the only passenger to disagree with him.

"Drive properly, may Allah guide you," he said, his face tense. "There is a police car following us"

Salim got the message. He turned sharply to the right, shot off the road, hit a boulder, reversed back onto the road and drove straight and sedately, sticking to his side so doggedly that his right tyres were off the tarmac altogether.

Two-tone blaring in mechanical donkey mode, the police car, which had been following them for the last mile, overtook them and blocked the road a hundred yards ahead. All hilarity and inebriation suddenly evaporated.

* * * *

Edward, Sa'd and Ahmed stayed in the minibus. Salim got out and walked slowly and unsteadily to the policemen, who were standing in the road beside their car. There were two of them; one was small, middle-aged, grim-faced and tight-lipped, the other young, slightly obese, with a pleasant, oafish face.

"What's your name?" the small policeman demanded in a Yemeni accent.

"Salim al Dosari," said Salim.

"Al Dosari! What are you doing with this foreigner? You come from a highly respected tribe. Why are you mixing with characters like this?"

"He's our teacher," Salim explained in a quavering voice. "Of course, we don't really like him very much but we find it useful to take him on trips like this so that we can practise our English."

The other policeman laughed approvingly. "Crafty devils," he said.

Edward, who could hear all this quite clearly, was stunned.

"Is that really why you've taken me on this trip?" he asked in an undertone.

"Of course not," whispered Ahmed. "Salim is just telling them the sort of things they like to hear. This is no time to be sensitive... unless you want to go to prison."

"You've been drinking, haven't you?" the small policeman said, staring at Salim accusingly.

"No," said Salim. "I never drink. I don't even smoke."

"Nonsense! You smell like a primus-stove. I'm taking you all to the station."

"I'm sorry. I lied to you slightly," said Salim. "But I've drunk very little... and none of my friends have drunk anything at all."

"I needn't ask you where you got the drink from," the policeman said with a cold sneer. "Practising your English... Huh!"

"If you think the Englishman gave me the drink, that's quite untrue," replied Salim. "And I can prove it."

"I don't see how you are going to do that... Come here you lot!" he called. "Get out and come here... all of you!"

The others disembarked obediently. The policeman took Salim's keys and drove the minibus onto the rough. A quick search revealed the remains of the second bottle of spirit.

"There you are," said Salim smugly. "He's innocent. Or do you think English people make their own hooch and sell it to Khajalis?"

"All right, so we'll just have to find out who you got this from," said the grim policeman.

"I'll tell you," Salim said. "I bought it from one of the Emir's sons. Would you like to know which one so you can go and arrest him? He's Sheikh..."

"Enough of that," the policeman blustered, darkening with embarrassment. "Anyway, you're in illegal possession of alcohol and that's a crime. Come on, all of you! Get into the car... No you fools! Not your car. Ours."

* * * *

Predictably, it was a gloomy ride. Ahmed stared miserably out of the window, muttering "My mother will kill me", until the fat policeman turned round and told him to shut up. Salim looked inscrutable. Edward pictured various scenarios for his deportation - being dragged through Passports handcuffed to a uniformed policeman and bundled unceremoniously onto a London-bound aeroplane, escorted to the departure gate by a grim-faced British Embassy official, or driven to the airport in a prison van and handed over to a gaggle of sarcastic air-hostesses.

* * * *

"I wish they'd tell us how much longer we've got to hang around," Salim muttered.

They had been taken under police escort to the hospital for blood-tests and were now in the police station reception area, where they had been waiting for a couple of hours under the not very watchful eye of a young constable. The duty-sergeant was sitting on the other side of a long counter cluttered with files, overflowing ashtrays and dirty tea glasses. Behind him was a metal cage occupied by a motley group including a depressed-looking Pakistani in *shalwar kameez*, a few men in Arab dress, a smart Egyptian in a suit and three ragged Iranian boys.

"Hello mister. How are you?" the boys chorused in English for the hundredth time.

"Quiet!" the sergeant yelled, turning round and glaring at them intimidatingly for the hundredth time. "You're worse than dogs! You'd think you'd tire of barking but you just go on and on."

The boys sniggered.

A policeman brought in a file and looked ominously at Edward. The sergeant took it and perused it briefly.

"Hospital report," he said. "Sa'd, you're OK. You can go now. Salim, Ahmed and Adwood, you've got alcohol in your blood."

"Good luck. I'll take my father's car and go straight to our campsite and pick up the others. I expect they're thinking we've had an accident," Sa'd whispered. He turned to the sergeant.

"Thank you sir," he said. "I hope my friends can leave soon too."

"They'll have to spend the night with this bunch," the sergeant replied, jerking his head towards the cage.

"What about Edward?" Salim asked. "He's allowed to drink."

"Yes. But he's not allowed to drink illegal alcohol," the sergeant said. "He'll have to sleep here. The officer is coming in the morning and will decide what to do with him and the rest of you."

*   *   *   *

"Hello brothers. What brings you here?" an amiable stool-pigeon inquired as they were trying to mark out some territory at the back of the cage.

"A small problem," Salim said coldly. "Nothing serious."

The man hung around for a while, then went away.

"We'd better not tell anyone we're here," said Salim.

"Yes," Ahmed agreed. "Not for the moment anyway. At least, not till it's unavoidable. For now we can let our families think we're still in the desert."

*   *   *   *

"The officer will see you now," a policeman announced at six the following morning. "Together. Come with me."

They were escorted to the officer's room. Behind a big desk sat a lieutenant in his late twenties who glanced at Edward with amusement and invited them all to sit down. Suddenly he noticed Salim and his face darkened with anger.

"What's this, Salim? Have you no self-respect?" he demanded. "What do you think your father's going to say when he hears about this?"

"I know, Ali. I assure you this has taught me a lesson," Salim replied, hiding his relief behind an expression of shame and sorrow. "Believe me..."

"That's enough! I'm not talking to you! You are shit! How can I do my job properly when I have members of my own family breaking the law? If I'd known you were involved in this business I would have refused to touch it... I'd like to see you locked up for a good long time. As it is, I suppose I shall have to cancel the case."

He scribbled a note to the duty-sergeant and ten minutes later they were climbing back into the minibus.

*   *   *   *

"Thank God. We're not even going to be that late for work ... even after we've gone home and changed," Edward said.

"Yes. We can't go to the Training Centre dressed like this," Salim agreed, looking at his grimy, ash-smeared thobe. "With any luck the bosses will just think we've overslept and we won't need to come up with convoluted excuses."

"They probably won't even think that because I doubt if they'll know. We've got English lessons till nine o'clock today and Mr. Roy won't say anything if we miss the first half hour. After all, he's used to us being a bit on the drag sometimes... especially after the weekend," Ahmed said. "In fact, we probably won't be any later than we would have been if we'd driven back from the desert first thing this morning as we originally planned."

"And with any luck nobody will notice my absence as long as I'm in before half past eight. The only visitors I ever get in my office in the early hours are you lot," Edward said.

"By the way, don't take my cousin Ali too seriously," Salim said. "He was only putting on a show because he had to in front of his colleagues. I know him well. He and I are really close friends and he won't say a word to my family."

*   *   *   *

As it turned out, Edward arrived at work over an hour late, though none of the Training Centre management spotted him sneaking surreptitiously into his office at half past eight. When he had finished showering and dressing and went out to find a taxi - usually a simple, straightforward matter involving, at most, no more than a five-minute wait - Sod's Law decided to rear its ugly head and he had to stand by the roadside for nearly half an hour before one turned up. As he was in a hurry to get to work, he jumped in without agreeing on a fare and when he reached his destination the driver demanded twenty-five riyals – more than double the usual price.

"Rubbish! What are you talking about? I never pay more than ten riyals... sometimes less. Though as we didn't agree a rate before we started I'll give you twelve," Edward conceded.

He handed the money to the driver, who threw it on the floor.

"Twenty-five!!"

"No. Twelve. Take it or leave it."

The driver seized Edward's nose in a firm grip and squeezed it hard.

"Ha! I can see tears in your eyes. It hurts, doesn't it? Now give me twenty-five!"

The driver was a large, muscular man with a massive Pathan turban and a fierce expression, so Edward decided it would be advisable to climb down. Somewhat ungraciously, he proffered the money, mumbling: "All right. Take it then. You are a thief, but what can I do?"

"WHAT did you say?"

"Oh, nothing. Never mind."

"Go to Hell, English bastard!"

The taxi drove off.

Edward crept into his office feeling angry and humiliated, but a cup of tea revived his spirits and the rest of his day was uneventful.

3.

PROMOTION

"O.K. So what now?" said Edward Holdsworth to himself.

It was mid-February 1976. His special assignment at Mottled Oil was coming to an end within the next few weeks, but when he tried to look beyond it, the only thing he could see was a blank wall. Although he had always believed that a proper career plan was a good thing, at least in theory, since joining the world of work the main events in his life had generally been unplanned and unexpected and in practice he usually operated on the Mr. Micawber principle of "something is bound to turn up".

When he first decided he would like to try living abroad, he applied on the spur of the moment for a teaching job in Nigeria, but after waiting around for several weeks and hearing nothing from Mr. Sunshine - the official who had interviewed him at the Nigerian High Commission - he eventually signed a respectable-looking contract with an Iraqi Christian from Basra called Nuri who happened to be visiting London to recruit new teachers, and found himself working under the radar at his unlicensed language school in Tehran.

His dubious legal status was revealed to him in the taxi on the way from Tehran airport to his new home, although his boss assured him it was just a minor administrative matter, "so don't you worry about it".

In his first letter home, Edward wrote: "Most of our school's income ends up in the pockets of middle-ranking education and labour ministry officials who return the favour by letting us carry on illegally. However, as they are all doing very well out of it they are in no hurry to help us become legal, so at the end of the month - if this month is anything to go by - there is not enough left in the coffers to pay the staff.

"On pay day we - that is to say, I and my colleague Tina (who arrived here the day before me) - went to Nuri's office to collect our salaries.

"'I'm going to be absolutely frank with you,' he told us. 'I'm afraid there isn't any money at the moment, but never mind. There ought to be some in the next few days. What about if you come round to our place for dinner this evening and we have a party? ... In the meantime, here are some *toman*s for your groceries and bus fares.' Then he gave us about £10 each in local money.

"He is a cheerful, genial chap - balding and middle-aged with a bit of a paunch - and his wife and two little boys treat Tina and me as members of the family. I suppose we really ought to be rather annoyed but we have both become very fond of him and find it impossible to get too cross, even when we are reduced to living on a diet of *seerabi* from the little stall in the street outside our building - as we have been doing this month while waiting to be paid; *seerabi* consists of stewed tripe floating in a cauldron of pungent brown cowpat soup seasoned with wisps of half-digested hay which you can smell from halfway down the street. The old man we buy it from hooks it up out of the slurry, snips it into strips with a pair of rusty shears and gives it to us in a soggy brown paper bag. Not surprisingly, it is incredibly cheap.

"Although we are illegal immigrants on tourist visas, Nuri has signed a contract with Iran Air and I have been detailed to teach basic English to their new ground staff and cabin crews for six hours a day at their training centre. Luckily, it is only a few minutes' walk away so I don't have to spend any money on transport.

"Another problem about this job is that Nuri is an Iraqi and relations between Iran and Iraq are rather fraught at the moment. Consequently, we are always finding strange men in suits and dark glasses sitting in parked cars outside the school. Nuri says they are mostly from the Iraqi embassy because his government are suspicious of any of their citizens who happen to be living in Iran, but we are also being spied on by secret agents from the local state security service, who presumably think he might be an Iraqi spy."

Edward never developed a taste for life in Tehran under those circumstances and after six months he was able to escape to Kuwait, where he walked straight into a job at the Monotone School. After a year in Kuwait City, he was transferred to their branch in Khajal to join a new training programme at Mottled Oil.

By the beginning of March 1976, as the end of his special assignment grew ever nearer, it finally dawned on Edward that unemployment might be imminent, so he called on Nicky Wood to discuss his future.

"Mottled won't be wanting me around next month so... any idea what's going to happen to me?" he asked.

"Good question," Nicky said. "I suppose you could teach for a few hours at the school, but your rent and salary would cost us more than you would be earning so it would have to be quite a temporary arrangement. I discussed your case last week with Freddy at Head Office and he suggested I should make you redundant and send you home. That would also make a big hole in our funds though, as well as being rather tough on you. How would you like to take over as my replacement? I'm leaving in a few weeks' time, as you know, and it doesn't look as if there are any candidates for the post so far."

"Me as branch manager? What a horrible idea. I'm sure I'd absolutely hate it," Edward said. "You know I'm useless at making decisions."

"True."

"And I'd be no good at negotiating fees, solving crises, battling with landlords, dealing with stroppy staff or socialising with expatriate personnel managers and the like. I'd be a nervous wreck after the first week."

"But on the plus side you know the people. You're on good terms with your colleagues and in any case there are really no other options. We have our full quotas of contract teachers and, as you say, Mottled won't extend your assignment. After all, they only took you on in the first place as a favour."

*　　*　　*　　*

So Edward became the new branch manager of Monotone Khajal and moved into the manager's flat.

The flat and the Khajal branch office were on the upper floor of the school. It was a large building - quite old by Khajali standards - in a sprawling garden with guava, lime, pawpaw and pomegranate trees, as well as a small transient population of rats, house sparrows and an occasional stray cat, and it belonged to a cousin of the Ruler who had recently moved to a new concrete palace on the outskirts of the city.

On either side of the school were super-sized modern villas with colonnaded porticos tiled with glittering colourful mosaics, while to the rear of the garden, in a large area of open ground with thorn bushes and a couple of sad-looking stray date palms, was a small

Baluchi shanty settlement of plywood, driftwood, corrugated iron and palm-frond shacks, surrounded by fenced enclosures housing goats, sheep and one or two donkeys.

The families who lived in the settlement had originally come over from the Makran coast in south-eastern Iran and had been in Khajal for years – in some cases for several generations. Although they were an underclass with no citizenship rights, the Khajali population did not see them as aliens in the same category as Indians, Pakistanis or Bangladeshis, or even Northern Arabs. Most of them wore Arab dress but, unlike the Khajalis, whose thobes were nearly always white, the Baluchis' thobes' were more often green, brown, blue, yellow or grey, or even dark red or purple - any colour, in fact, apart from scarlet or pink, which were regarded as effeminate. Also unlike the Khajalis, who invariably wore a white muslin (or occasionally patterned red) headcloth held in place with a thick black cord, the Baluchi men were commonly bare-headed. The women, whose faces were usually uncovered, wore brightly coloured dresses and head wraps.

Edward regularly exchanged greetings with them from afar while he sat out on his balcony in the cool spring evenings after work, listening to the bleating and braying of their animals and inhaling distant whiffs of wood-smoke from their cooking fires and faint aromas of meat stew, rice and freshly baked tandoori bread.

*　*　*　*

To begin with, he found the job of branch manager less demanding than he had expected. He no longer had to get up at dawn to be at Mottled Oil's Training Centre at six, unless one of the contract teachers was ill and he had to fill in for him. Breakfast in his flat was a leisurely affair and the office telephone rarely rang before nine. The busiest time of day was the afternoon and evening when the school had its English classes for paying students. Some of them were Khajali schoolchildren, but the majority were young adult expatriates from the northern Arab regions - mainly Egypt, Lebanon and Palestine - whose inadequate grasp of the language was holding them back in their careers.

Most of the classes were taught by contract teachers from Mottled Oil who still had some energy left after the day's work and wanted to earn a bit of overtime pay; there was also an elderly Scottish housewife called Jean with an endearingly vague manner and a broad Glasgow accent that intrigued and mystified her pupils in equal measure. Her husband worked at the airport but nobody seemed to know in what capacity. Even Jean herself was unsure, though she told her colleagues that he definitely had nothing to do with the technical side because he had no technical qualifications.

The first ripple to disturb Edward's peace of mind was prompted by a telephone call a week or so into his second month.

"Is this Mr. Nicholas John?" said a harsh voice in Arabic with a Yemeni accent.

"Mr. Nicholas John Wood? Nicky Wood? He doesn't live here anymore," Edward replied. "He left the country last month."

"When will he be back?"

"He isn't coming back. His job here has finished."

"Not coming back? That is not acceptable... This is the police. We are calling from the traffic court because he is late and we have been waiting for him for the last hour to appear for his case."

"I never knew he had a case... I doubt if he knew either. He never said anything to me about it. What's happened?"

"He had an accident six months ago and he will certainly have received a summons. Who are you anyway?"

"I've taken over from him as manager of the Monotone School."

"Well, the court is waiting now and if he is not there you will have to come instead. You must come at once... We are already running very late because of him."

"But this is a problem between him and you. What has it got to do with me?"

"You're English, aren't you? Same nationality as him? And you're living at his address? Come on! You're responsible now. You must appreciate that it doesn't make sense to have a court case with a judge and his staff waiting for an accused if the accused is nowhere to be found."

"I'm sorry but I can't come now. I'm busy," Edward protested.

"This is all very irregular. You haven't heard the last of it," the policeman said and hung up.

For the next few days Edward, who was an inveterate worrier, lived in fear of imminent arrest though his Khajali friends insisted that the offence of Guilt by Proxy did not exist on the Khajali statute books. Then towards the end of the following week the office telephone rang at eight in the morning.

"Mr Nicky?" said a voice in English.

"He's left. My name's Edward Holdsworth. Can I help you? I am his replacement," Edward said.

"This is Major Abdullah Kurdi from the CID. You are required here in my office immediately," said the voice.

"Oh God!" exclaimed Edward to himself, as his bowels began to churn with fright. "And I was beginning to think they had forgotten."

"Now?" he quavered.

"Yes, now. Now. I will see you in a few minutes."

Edward had never been to the CID before, though he knew where it was and that it was one of the ports of call that had to be visited when getting clearance for non-British teachers. (One hangover from Britain's imperial past in the Gulf was that British-born UK passport holders were exempted from the normal visa procedures, while other nationalities - including Americans and

Commonwealth citizens - had to obtain no-objection certificates and entry visas.)

Major Kurdi was a small, elderly Palestinian in a smart navy blue uniform. He welcomed Edward warmly, invited him to sit in the armchair beside his desk and ordered an underling to bring him a cup of tea.

"Nice to meet you. Mr. Nicky, your predecessor, was a good friend of mine and I am sure we will be friends too."

He produced an old copy of the *Daily Telegraph* and pointed at the Quick Crossword.

"Now," he said. "What about this? A word meaning edge. Five letters beginning with V."

"V? ... Verge would fit," Edward suggested. "Try verge."

"Thank you... I think that could be correct."

A uniformed constable appeared carrying a sheaf of official-looking papers and stood expectantly in the doorway.

"Go away," said Major Kurdi sharply. "Can't you see I'm busy?" The constable withdrew smirking.

"And what about this one?" the major continued. "Dairy product. Six letters. The second letter is H. I think the last one might be an E."

"Erm... Cheese?" said Edward.

"Hmm... Cheese... Hmm... Yes... Very possibly... Thank you... I think we can leave that for the present. I'll call you later if I need any help with the rest... Now... More tea?"

"No thanks. I've already had quite a lot of tea this morning."

The major rummaged through a pile of papers on his desk and extracted a page of neatly handwritten copperplate English. "I am writing a letter to Mr. Billings, my old English commanding officer in the Palestine Police, to wish him the compliments of the season. He is now retired and living in Rhodesia. Could you please cast an eye over it and let me know if my English is correct?"

"Perfect," said Edward a few minutes later. "Though I might phrase this sentence a little bit differently. You've written: 'I miss those happy days and I would be superbly delighted to see your jolly face again and chew the fat'. Nicely idiomatic, but how about something like: 'I have very fond memories of those days and would love to see you again and talk about old times'."

"You think that's better?"

"Yes, I think so."

"All right... I'll change it. And the rest of the letter?"

"It looks absolutely fine to me."

"My English is good, isn't it?"

"Excellent. Better than mine."

"Ha-ha. You flatter me... Anyway, thank you... That would seem to be all for now. I don't think I need detain you any longer. It has been very good to make your acquaintance and you have been a great help. Come and see me again whenever you like and if there is anything I can do for you, just let me know."

"Thanks. Actually, there is one matter I am going to have to deal with soon. We are planning to bring a new teacher out and as he has an Australian passport I think he will need approval from your department."

"Of course. No problem at all. Just bring me the details and I'll sort it all out for you."

They parted with expressions of mutual goodwill.

*   *   *   *

Some days later Edward took Major Kurdi up on his offer and returned to his office with the application forms for Jim Barrett - the new Australian teacher Monotone had recently recruited in London to work on the Mottled Oil contract. (Following a recent directive from the Ruler's Palace that they must train and employ more Khajali nationals, the Mottled management had given Monotone emergency instructions for an extra English teacher to be brought out as soon as possible.) He saw that the major was alone at his desk, so he knocked at the door and walked straight in with a breezy "Good morning".

The major looked up from his perusal of the local daily paper and frowned.

"Yes?" he snapped irritably. "Who are you? What do you want?"

"I visited you a week or so ago and you told me you could help me with an application," said Edward.

"No, it wasn't me. I've never seen you before in my life. What application? You must have been talking to someone else."

"No, it was you," Edward insisted gently. "You gave me a cup of tea and we discussed some crossword clues."

"Crossword clues? *Crossword* clues?" the major was silent for a few moments as he sorted through his memories of recent events in his life. "Aha." He broke into a smile. "Yes of course... You're the new manager of that language school. Have you had a haircut?"

"Not recently, but I am wearing a different-coloured shirt today."

"Ah, that must be it. Sorry, my friend. I didn't recognize you for a moment. Now what can I do for you?"

"Our school wants to bring out a new English teacher. He's living in London, but he has an Australian passport so he will need a visa. I haven't done this before but I understand that I have to get a No Objection Certificate for him from the CID."

"Yes. That's right... One minute." He summoned a constable from the outer office.

"Take this Englishman to have his forms checked, then make sure he gets all the right signatures and stamps."

An hour later Edward emerged from the building with a fistful of signed and stamped papers and took a taxi to the Passports and Immigration Department, where he was told that the official he needed to see was out because he had had to take his wife to the hospital. Edward would probably find him in if he came back later, "though tomorrow morning might be better. Probably. Best if you come after ten".

*   *   *   *

Although they were renowned for their easy-going work practices, which even their own staff conceded were towards the slothful end of the relaxed spectrum, Immigration were surprisingly prompt once they had received the papers and just over a week later Jim Barrett's visa was ready.

The man himself arrived a few days after that and Edward collected him from the airport. He had some difficulty recognizing him as he approached the Arrivals gate because he looked at least ten years older than the photograph on his application form and considerably more tattered and torn (he was forty-one, according to his passport, but from his appearance he could have been well over fifty), and his eyes had a squiffy look which suggested that he had indulged unstintingly in the airline's hospitality throughout the six and a half hour flight.

He was a short, squat man with a shock of dark brown tousled hair liberally sprinkled with grey and wore a faded tartan shirt and grey flannel trousers. He was sweating profusely because he was also wearing a bomber jacket and Khajal Airport was a lot hotter than Heathrow or the aeroplane. When, with a forced smile and sinking heart, Edward had identified him and introduced himself, hoping against hope that in this case first impressions were misleading, Barrett nodded, befuddledly.

"Must go for a piss. Where is it?" he said. Edward pointed him towards a sign marked "Toilets" in Arabic and English. He lurched off and reappeared a few minutes later.

"I'm putting you in a flat with Steve Kettle, one of your

colleagues you'll be working with at Mottled Oil," Edward told him as they set off towards the town in an airport taxi. "...You'll like him," he added hopefully.

"Hmm."

"He's an interesting character," Edward persisted, as he tried to establish some kind of rapport with his new employee. "He's the oldest member of our staff and he came quite late to teaching after a decade as a businessman in West Africa..."

"How old is he?"

"Forty-four... No, I think he has just had a birthday. He must be forty-five, but actually he looks older because he's a bit overweight – middle-age spread, you know - and nearly bald... and what little hair he has left is quite grey... He's got a lot of Khajali friends, so you'll be able to meet some local people."

"I don't think I'll be wanting to socialise with the locals unless I have to as part of the job." Jim grunted before lapsing into silence for a few moments. "...Now this Steve or whatever his name is who I'm supposed to be shacking up with tonight... Not married? No little woman back in the UK?"

"No. I suppose you could call him a confirmed bachelor."

"I see" (enigmatic sniff).

"...Well, I expect you would probably like something to eat now before we go to the flat, so what about if I take you to the Strand?" Edward suggested brightly. "The food's not fantastic, but it's quite a decent place... You know, clean... smartish... and it has professional-looking Lebanese waiters in starched white jackets. Apart from the dining room at the Khajal Palace Hotel, which is where most foreign businessmen stay, it's the only place in this country where you can get a Western-style meal."

"OK, OK, but listen... about my accommodation... I'm prepared to flat-share for a few days if you insist, but not on a permanent basis. Eventually I'll be wanting a place of my own."

"Didn't they tell you in London that teachers on bachelor status have to share? Of course, if you want to rent your own place and pay for it yourself, that's up to you," said Edward nervously.

"I don't remember them saying anything like that. We'll have to sort that out. In any case, you can't expect me to rent my own place. Apart from the fact that I haven't got any money, my contract says I'm entitled to free furnished accommodation..." He scowled and looked accusingly at Edward. "Still, we can talk about it after we've eaten. We'll leave it for the moment."

"It's the Monotone rule. It's not my decision," Edward explained.

"But you're the manager here. You ought to be able to do something about it."

"Well, I can't. I'm sorry."

*   *   *   *

"Hmm... Stormy weather ahead," Edward said to himself as they tucked into their braised lamb and tinned peas at the Strand and Jim commented unfavourably on the quality of the cuisine. "I wish it was in my nature to be a bit more of a leader and a bit less apologetic. After all, even though he is my subordinate, he is behaving as if he is the boss, not me... I'll have to stick to my guns about the flat... but I expect he'll carry on kicking when I do... Still, even at the risk of a confrontation I'll have to make it absolutely clear to him that his contract doesn't entitle him to a place of his own at our expense."

As it turned out, the storm Edward had predicted arrived from a different direction altogether. Its earliest rumblings began immediately after Jim had given his first lesson to his new class - a small group of middle-aged mechanics from Mottled Oil's Marine Department.

"We can't understand this man," one of them said to Roy Sladen, the senior teacher, later than morning.

"Really? Why not? He's Australian but he talks more or less like us," Roy replied.

"He was tell us about behind and in front of - of course we know about that already, but then he say in front of is sometimes behind. When we ask him what he mean he just write 'IN FRONT OF IS SOMETIMES BEHIND' on the blackboard. We ask him again and he say 'I already told you.'"

"Those men have got lazy minds and it's clear that their intellects need stretching. I think it's important they grasp the idea of relativity," Jim explained when Roy suggested a less complicated approach might be preferable. "And I've got no time for baby talk and what do you call them? ... visual aids and infantile things like that."

"But look," Roy pleaded. "Don't think I'm dictating to you. That's not my style. I'm sure you're an experienced teacher and know what you're doing, but the men in your class just need to be able to communicate in basic English. That's all. Most of them have never been to school – not even primary school - and it's a bit late now to start teaching them philosophical concepts."

Roy had been teaching in oil companies in the Gulf and North Africa for nearly ten years. He was now in his early thirties – a rather academic-looking man with a personable manner, dark receding hair and a permanently mild expression who was popular with his colleagues and students. As well as enjoying a well-deserved reputation as the most gifted teacher on the Mottled Oil contract, he was also respected for his tact and diplomatic skills, including an ability to nip nascent problems in the bud.

However, he failed to convince Jim Barrett.

"I'm not a thicko, you know," Jim retorted truculently. "I know what I'm doing. Best if you leave me to handle things my way."

*   *   *   *

"London has done it again", Jim's new colleagues concluded at the end of his first day.

Over the previous three years London had sent Khajal several unsatisfactory teachers because Freddy - their boss at Head Office - was more interested in cheapness than quality and, it was claimed, often used to "just hook people in from off the street and give them an air ticket". ("Excellent news, Edward/Nicky etc.! We've got the ideal man for you here. Bags of enthusiasm and that's much more important than qualifications. I'm sure he'll get the hang of it once you put him in a classroom.") On previous occasions the bargain-basement teachers had usually managed to survive undetected by Mottled's Personnel Department for several weeks, or even months, though none had made it to the end of their one-year contracts and this meant that they actually cost a lot more than a better paid, better qualified recruit would have done.

So although it was almost certain Jim Barrett would have to go eventually, the odds were that Mottled would not spot him immediately as a dud.

The rest of the week was fairly uneventful. The mechanics grumbled that they were wasting their time and not learning anything, but Roy promised them he would sort something out and persuaded them to wait before taking their complaints to the management. Back at the flat, Steve Kettle found Jim a quiet, if rather surly, housemate and told Edward that on the evidence so far he could probably live with him.

However, he changed his mind a few days later.

* * * *

It was evening and Steve was in the sitting room with a couple of Khajali guests when Jim walked in, threw a venomous glance in their direction and sat down in a vacant armchair without saying a word.

"This is my new colleague Jim. He arrived this week and he is sharing the flat with me," Steve said.

"Nice to meet you Mr. Jim. How are you?" the visitors inquired.

"Well," Jim replied, glaring at them. "Where can I begin? ... I'm well enough. I'm not ill, but that's about all I can say... Believe me, I've been around and I've seen some godawful places but this one takes the biscuit. Know what I mean? ... I've been in Cadgel a few days and from what I've seen so far, the people in charge here couldn't organise a piss-up in a brewery. They certainly don't know how to run a country... Not a clue... Understand what I'm saying?"

"I think you're saying you don't like it here," the older of the guests said, visibly shocked at Jim's blatant lack of courtesy. "Why did you come to Khajal then?"

"I have my reasons, but I'm not going to spell them out now." He stood up and headed for the door.

"You'll know soon enough," he added with an ominous look and stalked out of the room mumbling to himself.

"Sorry about that," Steve said, looking rather flustered. "To be honest, I'm worried that he might not be quite right in the head."

"Yes. Little bit crazy," the visitors agreed.

*　　*　　*　　*

At the Training Centre the next morning, Jim's group of Marine Department mechanics burst into the staffroom half way through the first lesson and announced in dramatic tones that there was an "emergency please come quick". Luckily, it was Roy Sladen's free period so they had someone to listen to them as they explained:

"Mr. Jim threw a chair at Nasser... Yes! ... Yes, a chair... And he shooted at us... Now he is curled up on the floor... His eyes are open but he is refuse to speak."

"What happened?" Roy asked.

"Nasser told him his lessons are not useful for us. Then Mr. Jim shooted that we are all counts and he said some other bad words. Nasser told to him he is without polite and he threw a chair at him."

"You go and get a cup of tea and I'll see what I can do," Roy said.

He went into the classroom and found Jim sitting in the teacher's chair looking blankly at an empty classroom.

"I'm going to take you to the doctor," he said.

"No need. I'm perfectly OK but I refuse... positively refuse to have any more to do with that lot."

"I'm sorry, but we must get the doctor to check you out. I insist. We can discuss all the other matters later."

He took Jim to the company clinic, which was next door to the training centre, and handed him over to Khalil - the Palestinian male nurse. The doctor was free, so he was able to see Jim immediately. Roy returned to the training centre and rang Edward to tell him what had happened. Recognizing that this was almost certainly a real emergency that required his presence, Edward reluctantly abandoned his coffee, toast and waking-up-to-the-world music and set off for the Mottled compound. Just after he arrived, there was a call from Khalil at the clinic summoning him and Roy to the doctor's office immediately.

"Your man cannot be allowed anywhere near a classroom," the doctor informed them. "He is very sick - I mean seriously ill - and I have called for an ambulance to take him to the Sheikh Khalid Hospital."

"What do you think is wrong with him?" Edward inquired.

"He is suffering from dangerous delusions. When he first came in and I asked him how he was feeling he said that he had been grievously insulted by a bunch of rats and traitors and he was going to punish them severely. I asked him to explain and he said he was going to make sure they were put on trial and executed or flogged to within an inch of their lives. He was quite matter-of-fact about it. Not in a towering rage or anything. I asked him how he could have them put on trial and he said that he was the rightful ruler of Khajal and could do anything he liked. Although I was afraid he wasn't joking, I smiled and he yelled at me and told me to show him some respect... Anyway, after I had talked to him a bit more I realised he was being deadly serious... Of course I have had to call Personnel and George Weever should be here any minute."

Edward was aghast and his face took on a greyish tinge.

"OK," he said shakily. "I'll hang on and wait for George. Roy, I think somebody ought to go in the ambulance with Jim. Could you go?"

"Well," Roy said. "Actually I think it would probably be better if you went with Jim and I spoke to George because he will want to know what we are going to do about the training programme now that we are a teacher short. Though obviously you will have to see George some time... if for no other reason than to apologise on Monotone's behalf and reassure him that Jim will be replaced as soon as possible."

Edward agreed and accompanied Jim to the Sheikh Khalid Hospital where he checked him in and signed a paper confirming that Monotone was the patient's sponsor. Then he returned to Mottled Oil, where he had an awkward meeting with Weever.

"Although I'm not blaming you personally, old chap," the Personnel Manager told him, "you have to admit that Monotone's credibility has sunk to around zero now. Don't they have any recruitment checks at your London office? This fellow - what's his name, Barrett - should have been flagged up before he signed a contract. Even if his teaching references are phoney... and even if they were accepted without question, his mental unfitness should have been spotted at his medical... Assuming that they do give their new teachers a medical?"

"I can't understand it. Perhaps he conned Head Office by

presenting them with a phoney medical certificate," Edward said. (Though he himself had not been given a medical before joining Nuri's outfit or Monotone and he had no idea whether or not a medical examination was part of the London recruitment procedure.)

"Anyway," Weever said. "The main thing is, what is to be done now? You'll have to get a replacement as soon as possible." He smiled wryly. "And by replacement I mean a proper, sane, qualified teacher who speaks good, intelligible English. Another disaster like this and we'll have to scrap our agreement with you. We'll have every legal right to do so. And correct me if I'm wrong, but I think that here in Cadgel, Monotone depends on us for its survival. I doubt if it could carry on with just the school and one or two little government teaching contracts?"

"It would be a bit of a struggle," Edward agreed, wondering how long it would be before he had to start looking for another job himself.

He returned to the school and had a long telephone conversation with the London office.

"Stop panicking Edward," Freddy told him. "I can tell you're panicking. I can hear it in your voice. Well, don't. We've got an ideal replacement ready to travel out to Khajal in the next two days. British born, so he won't need a visa, and he's got good qualifications. The only reason I didn't send him to you before was that I thought he was over-qualified. He's a Scot, but he hasn't got an accent and he's had loads of experience."

* * * *

The Sheikh Khalid Hospital was a grand-looking, rambling old building near the seafront a stone's throw from the Emir's Palace and most of its inmates were from the upper end of the social scale. (Less well connected mental patients were usually incarcerated in a sort of cage below the "*Qala'ah*" - the old hill-top fort that housed the headquarters of the security services, armed forces and police as well as the country's gold reserves - where they could be seen and chatted to by passers-by and the general public and provided entertainment for some of the less praiseworthy elements of the local youth on their days off.) The next day, Edward went to the hospital to see how Jim Barrett was getting on. He found him in good spirits.

"This place is great," Barrett said. "Almost perfect. Not quite as luxurious as some of the other places I've lived in, but at least the people here recognize me for what I am and treat me with due deference and respect. This morning I had a long discussion with my Protocol Man– you know, that Arab bloke in the office down the corridor... you've probably seen him - and I told him I was quite happy to leave the other fellow in charge of the country for the moment - as acting Emir or Regent. He said that was a wise decision."

"I see. Is there anything you need? Anything I can get you?" Edward asked.

"I wouldn't mind some Havana cigars. I thought I'd go out and see if I could find some this morning, but my guards - those men at the gate in the blue uniforms - suggested it would be better if I stayed here in my palace and one of them escorted me back here to my stateroom. They're really spot-on about ensuring my personal security, which is right and proper when you consider who I am."

The "Protocol Man" (a jolly Egyptian in his sixties who introduced himself to Edward as Barrett's "assigned psychiatrist") told Edward his patient was fit to travel but only with an escort. Freddy in London told Edward to accompany Jim back to England - preferably on the next available flight – and agreed that, as the new teacher was booked to travel out within the next couple of days, Roy should receive him at the airport and help him settle in till Edward returned. Meanwhile, he (Roy) would also take over temporarily as acting manager while continuing to run the English classes at the Mottled Training Centre.

Back in Khajal after his lightning trip to London, Edward wrote to his girlfriend:

"...Of course I've already told you most of my harrowing story. I had one final scare, thanks to Roy and the new teacher, whose name by the way is Dick... As soon as I got back to Khajal I went to see Roy and asked him if Dick had arrived safely and what he thought of him.

"He's very pleasant and friendly but I think the trainees may have a problem understanding him. Rather a strong Scottish accent and he's got a bit of a cleft palate. Anyway, let's go and see him now. He's looking forward to meeting you," Roy said.

"As you can imagine, I was overcome with dread, but we went round to the flat where I was greeted by this beaming middle-aged man who held out his hand to me and said:

"'I'm reet pleekhd ti be meet'n ye Mikhter Holdkhsworlkh.'

"I tried to smile and welcomed him to Monotone Khajal, but my face must have registered unmitigated horror. Then he and Roy both burst out laughing.

"'Don't worry. I don't normally talk like that,' he said in perfect received pronunciation English. 'And please don't blame Roy. I'm afraid this was my idea after he told me about what has been happening here recently.'

"Now that I've had a chance to look through Dick's CV in more detail I see that he was actually a part-time announcer on the forces radio when he was with the army in Berlin in the sixties and he also has ten years' experience as a teacher of English as a foreign language in France and Germany, so I'm hoping life will be plain sailing from now on."

*   *   *   *

The "Barrett Saga" became a *cause celebre* in the Monotone annals (it subsequently became known as "The Episode of the Antipodean Turd") and there was considerable speculation about whether Jim truly believed his own bizarre claim that he was the rightful ruler of Khajal. He had no love or sympathy for the Khajalis, he spoke no Arabic and what he knew about the country and its history and culture could be written on the back of a postage stamp.

"What I suspect," Steve said, "is that he was probably just raving randomly when he first made the claim in the Mottled clinic, because he had lost his rag completely. Then when he realised the doctor was recording his statement, he decided to stick with it and bluff it out as he didn't want to look even more of a fool than he really was. Whatever the truth of the matter, he had a very twisted and confused mind. That's for sure... I wish I could have felt sorry for him but he was such a fundamentally unlikeable person. A really nasty piece of work."

4.

BUMPS ON THE ROAD

Dick Brown, Barrett's replacement, had been at Mottled Oil for just over a week and he was settling in well. His colleagues and students liked him and George Weever, the Personnel Manager, had been heard to say that he was "a refreshing change from some of the weird types their London people too often send out to teach our trainees". Dick himself was quietly happy with the job, though in private he was scathing about the Company's patronisingly colonial attitude to "the Cadgerlies".

He had never been in the Middle East before and he had come across very few Arabs when he was teaching English in France and Germany, but he and his group of young Khajali clerical trainees hit it off from the start. Although they often found English a challenge - few of them had had much formal schooling before joining the Company - they were generally easy-going, friendly and keen to learn, and they were never offended by his ill-concealed mirth when their wires got crossed.

"Do you know what conflicts are?" he asked his new class the first morning when they were trying to untangle a passage in their comprehension book.

"Conflicts? Yes of course. English people have them for breakfast with milk and sugar."

One of the trainees, a teenager called Sa'id, was obsessed with new English words and presented Dick with a daily list before the first lesson of the day. He was basically a cheerful, good-natured lad, though when he spoke English he sounded uncouth and he often came across as brusque and hectoring:

"Look here Mr. Dick."

"Yes, Sa'id. What is it?"

"What does this word mean?" (jabbing his forefinger at a scrawl at the top of the paper).

"Burow? Um... You probably mean burrow. Double r. It's a hole where a rabbit lives."

"No it isn't. I think it looks like a table."

"Bureau perhaps? B -U -R -E - A- U? It can mean a desk or an office."

"Which one?"

"Either."

"What's the opposite of buroo?"

"There isn't an opposite."

"So you don't know. Write the spelling here... And... this word?"

"This one? Fowl?"

"Yes. What is it?"

"It can be another word for a chicken."

"I see... So we cook our food in the fowl."

"Sorry. I'm not with you. What do you mean?"

"Chicken. The place where we cook."

"No. That's a kitchen. A chicken is a bird. You know, a bird you can eat."

"What's the opposite of fowl?"

"What are you going to do with all these words? ... I know...

You're planning to be Khajal's answer to Roget, aren't you?"

"What's a Roget?"

"Never mind. Ask me again later."

Tariq, the youngest member of the group, was a fan of Western pop songs:

"Do you like Arthur Cat, Mr. Dick?"

"I don't think I've met him. Which department is he in?"

"No. Not a man. Lady. American singer. Black."

"Mmm... Arthur Cat... Black American singer... Oh! ... You mean Eartha Kitt."

"Yes. That's what I said. Arthur Cat."

"Eartha Kitt. Yes. I quite like some of her songs."

"I like black American singers."

"Me too. But not all of them."

"What about Elephant Gerald?"

"Who?"

"Elephant Gerald. She's black too. She's an old."

"Oh Ella! Ella Fitzgerald! Yes, I love her. She's wonderful."

*   *   *   *

Peter Frazer, Edward's old housemate from the days when they were teachers together, was the youngest Monotone employee on the Mottled Oil contract and, according to his more seasoned colleagues, this sometimes showed.

"He's basically amiable, decent and hard-working. However, although there is no malice in him, his sense of humour is often mischievous and tactless. He can also be prickly at times and he has a tendency to grumble and put his prejudices (which are legion) on display on occasions when silence would be more prudent. This can put people's backs up - particularly the backs of those who don't know him well," Edward wrote in his confidential staff assessment report. "Those who do know him well like him and invariably forgive him when he behaves in a way that others might regard as offensive or lacking in good taste."

Unlike the majority of Western expatriates in the Gulf, Peter's motives for joining Monotone in Khajal were not so much pecuniary as due to a desire to see the world and enjoy the opportunities for excitement and adventure that he felt Arabia would have to offer.

He was the only Mottled Oil English teacher who owned a car and he had recently started a trial arrangement under which he would pick up his colleagues from home and give them a lift to and from work in exchange for a modest monthly payment. This system, which had been working satisfactorily for the past few weeks, was more reliable than the alternatives - a haphazard municipal bus service with no regular timetable, or taxis that were sometimes few and far between, particularly at the times when they were most needed.

While they were on their way home from work one afternoon, a young Pathan labourer stepped off the narrow pavement into the path of Peter's car and was knocked down. Fortunately, the road was clogged with traffic and the car was crawling at about ten miles an hour, but the boy's head hit the tarmac and he lay on the road in a daze, bleeding spectacularly from a severe-looking gash on his forehead and scalp.

A crowd of his Pathan co-workers surrounded the car and Peter and his passengers got out to wait for the police and the emergency services. Within a few minutes an ambulance arrived with sirens blaring and lights flashing and the victim was rushed to Khajal General Hospital. By the time the police appeared most of the crowd had begun to disperse, though some of the bystanders who had witnessed the incident were waiting to report what they had seen and insisted that the Englishman had been driving like a maniac and was "probably drunk".

Peter and his passengers were ushered into the police car and driven to the Traffic Police Headquarters, where they were shown into a small room to wait for a senior officer to arrive and decide what to do with them.

"The only one of you who is being detained is the driver, but we will want statements from all of you," the young constable guarding them explained.

"What's going to happen now?" Peter inquired.

"You'll be seen by Captain Dirgham. He was appointed last year to replace Commander Bob Wilkins, the Englishman who used to be head of the traffic police."

Captain Dirgham, who arrived shortly before sunset, was a large, breezy, middle-aged Palestinian who spoke fluent idiomatic English. He called them into his office, ordered glasses of sweet tea and got down to business.

"Before we start, you should call your boss, or manager, or whoever it is that is in charge of you," he said.

"He'll be busy at the moment. Can't we go home and tell him after we have given our statements and you've finished with us?" Peter Frazer asked.

"No. Sorry my friend. Out of the question... Look... Apologies if I'm wrong but I get the feeling you don't understand how serious this is. And just how serious your own situation might be. This is not just a little speeding or parking offence and it is quite possible that you - I mean you, the driver - may not be going home at all today. We've been told the boy is in a critical condition and there could be criminal charges. The rest of you can go when we have finished with you, but there are procedures we have to go through including checks on your residence status, and your boss will have to come and explain officially who you all are and what you are doing in this country."

Edward Holdsworth was manning the reception desk at the

school and when the call came through he was wondering why his Mottled teachers had failed to turn up for their classes.

"Hi Edward. Sorry. Peter here. I'm afraid we're in a bit of bother. We've had an accident and we're at the police headquarters and... well, it looks like we might be here for some time. The officer in charge says you need to come down and vouch for us and I think he wants you to bring some kind of documentary proof that we're here legally."

"Well, that's a bit of a problem as I don't imagine it's your personnel files he's after and I haven't got your passports. Presumably none of you have them with you, or any other form of ID?"

"Apart from my driving licence I don't think any of us are carrying proof of identity."

Leaving the school's part-time accountant to man the desk, Edward took a taxi to the Traffic Police and explained to Captain Dirgham that all his teachers were *bona fide* Monotone employees, but that their passports were in their lodgings.

"OK," the Captain said. "So what I'll do is... I'll take some statements now and then they can all go home. Including you, Peter Frazer. But you must bring your passports in tomorrow morning so we can confirm who you are and that you are here legally."

In the end, it was decided that transcribing statements from the driver and all his passengers would take too long, so the Captain agreed that just two statements would probably be sufficient - one from Peter and one from a passenger (who it was agreed should be Roy Sladen as he was the senior teacher). These would be translated into Arabic and Peter and Roy would sign the Arabic and English copies after they had been typed up the following day.

News of the accident had already reached Mottled Oil before sunrise the next day. Khajal was a small place and news travelled fast, especially when Westerners were involved in anything remotely dramatic, scandalous or criminal. George Weever had heard most of the details from a friend with a contact in the police and was, as Edward expected, annoyed ("Yet another Monotone cock-up") because he feared it was likely to disrupt the classes at the training centre. The technical and clerical trainees were also aware of what had happened; they were invariably abreast of the latest gossip though it was not always accurate by the time it reached them. In this instance their sympathies were coloured mainly by their personal opinions of Peter, Westerners and Pathans, as well as the version of events they had heard.

"Mr. Peter is not a child. He is certainly old enough to know that he is not a racing driver, but he seems to think his old Peugeot's a McLaren or a Ferrari," said Saleh, the training centre's sole Bedouin technical trainee. Although he was not curmudgeonly by nature, he had an ingrained suspicion of the *Ingiliz* and their motives for being in his country and believed that the Pathan witnesses, as fellow Muslims, were more likely to be telling the unvarnished truth. Sa'd and Salim, on the other hand, sided firmly with Peter, whom they saw as a friend in need. Of the others, the majority were inclined more towards the pro-Peter camp, though they had some reservations.

*   *   *   *

A few weeks later a summons arrived through the post instructing Peter to attend the Traffic Court "in person" on a Sunday morning the following month, so he immediately told Edward, who arranged to accompany him.

"Apart from anything else," Edward said as they set off on the morning of the hearing, "I feel I ought to be there to remind you to treat the court with a bit of respect. When you were at the police HQ after the accident it seemed to me that your attitude left something to be desired. As if you saw yourself as being in some way above the law because you are British."

"I'm sorry if I gave that impression. I think I tend to react that way when I am feeling nervous. And I was nervous because I know the law here is tougher than it is at home - in theory anyway, even though of course in practice the whole Khajali system somehow feels pretty casual. Remember how you and the trainees were released from the police lock-up without charge when the officer on duty turned out to be Salim's cousin."

The Traffic Court was a modest-looking office in the central court complex. The judge - a chubby, bald, bespectacled Egyptian in a suit - was sitting behind a large desk piled high with files and bundles of papers, chatting to a young Palestinian clerk in jeans and a tee-shirt. The only other person in the room was a uniformed policeman sitting on a collapsible chair by the door with a sub-machine gun on the floor beside him.

Peter presented his summons to the judge, who passed it to the clerk, who then rummaged through the documents and papers and produced a file with numbers and notes in Arabic and the English word "FREEZER" in large letters on the cover.

"Mr. Freezer?" the judge enquired.

"Yes," said Peter.

Sometimes it is appropriate to correct a foreigner's spelling and pronunciation and sometimes it is not. As Peter's tactlessness and indiscretion were legendary, Edward gave a silent sigh of relief when he opted for the latter course.

"Right," said the judge in English. "I have studied all the witness statements with regard to your case and I have concluded that you were probably not speeding or driving recklessly. However, it is also clear that the accident would not have happened if you had been paying as much attention as you should have been. Luckily, the boy wasn't too badly hurt. His skull wasn't fractured, but even so it would be setting a bad example if I let you go away... ha-ha...

Scotch-free. (Is that the expression?) Have you anything to say before I give my decision?"

"Only that I am very sorry, sir, and that I promise to be more careful in future," Peter replied in an uncharacteristically contrite and respectful tone.

"Then my ruling is that you must pay a fine of eight hundred riyals. You can pay it to the accounts department now. Otherwise, if you have not got your cheque book or the money with you, you must settle within seven days. Thank you... That will be all... You may leave now." The clerk wrote the verdict on a slip of paper and the judge signed and stamped it and handed it to Peter, who took it to the accounts department and wrote out a cheque for eight hundred riyals.

"That's nearly half a month's salary!" he grumbled as they headed for the car.

"Well at least it's over... and it could have been worse," Edward said. "Can you drop me off at the school on your way back to Mottled?"

*   *   *   *

As it turned out, it was not quite over. Five weeks later a letter arrived from the Shariah Court summoning Peter to attend a session on the morning of the following Tuesday "in connection with a claim for compensation by Mr. Fazal Yusufzai, nationality Pakistani ".

The court room was in a building near the city's fish market. It was a spacious hall with thick Persian carpets and heavy brocade-upholstered thrones round the walls, most occupied, mainly by Khajalis. There was a delicate aroma of *'oodh* (aloe wood) smoke in the air and Khajali attendants in Arab dress drifted to and fro, stopping from time to time to pour out tiny splashes of cardamom-flavoured coffee from beaked copper pots into shallow little handleless china cups, which they handed to favoured visitors and litigants. The presiding judge - Sheikh Ibn Sakhr - was ensconced behind a gigantic desk conferring in an undertone with a couple of animated old men who sat in front of him on leather chairs glaring at each other.

After a few minutes they were dismissed and another couple was called forward to sit in the judge's presence, while the first pair sat waiting to be summoned back for further discussions or to hear the verdict. This happened repeatedly and it was clear that several cases were being heard simultaneously. Ibn Sakhr was a portly old man in his late sixties with a slyly humorous face disfigured by large white patches on his cheeks, forehead and hands. He wore the standard garb of a religious sheikh - a plain white robe, a brown cloak and a heavy red and white shawl draped over his head without the traditional black headband.

An usher showed Peter and Edward to a couple of thrones and they were served cups of unsweetened coffee. (As Westerners they were treated as being in the "favoured" category.) A young Palestinian in shirt and trousers came over and joined them.

"I'm your translator," he explained. "Unless you'd prefer to conduct your case in Arabic yourselves."

"Thanks. I'm afraid our Arabic isn't up to it," Edward said. "Do you work for the court?"

"Yes. It's quite an interesting job. They're doing civil cases today - you know, disputes, compensation, that sort of thing, which can sometimes be a bit boring and complicated. I prefer the criminal cases. I understand you are here to answer a claim against you. Where is the other party?"

Fazal Yusufzai, nationality Pakistani, was sitting on a throne on the other side of the room with a small group of Pathans. He was a thin, sad-looking youth in his late teens with a shaven head, dressed in a traditional *kurta* pyjama suit and gold-embroidered leather sandals.

For the next hour Sheikh Ibn Sakhr summoned, dismissed and resummoned cases, during which he delivered occasional verdicts in tones that were inaudible to the rest of the room above the buzz of conversation and the clink of coffee cups. Eventually he beckoned to Peter and an usher led Fazal up to his desk.

"What's the problem?" he enquired.

"This boy was injured in a road accident when he was hit by a car driven by this Englishman and he is asking for compensation," a clerk explained, placing an open file before the judge.

"What was the injury?"

"A bad cut on the head and some bruises."

"I see. Let him show me the cut." The Sheikh gestured to Fazal, who leant over the desk so that the damage could be inspected. "...Oh... it is a bit faint now but still clearly visible. When did the accident happen?"

"A little over two months ago."

"So it could have been quite serious at the time. Bring me the tape measure."

The court tape measure was produced and the length of the cut was recorded as being just under ten centimetres.

"Alright," said Sheikh Ibn Sakhr. "Go and sit down now and I'll call you back in due course."

After another wait and several more cups of coffee, the judge beckoned Peter and Fazal back to hear the judgement.

"What's his name?" he asked, pointing at Peter.

"Frazer," the Palestinian translator said. "Nationality British."

"Freezer?" the judge laughed. "Funny name. Perhaps one of his ancestors made refrigerators. They call it a freezer in their language too, don't they?"

Everyone smiled politely, including Peter.

Then the judge issued his ruling.

"You must pay Fazal Yusufzai, nationality Pakistani, compensation totalling nine hundred and fifty riyals," the translator told Peter.

"Ha! Lucky you didn't poke his eye out," the judge chuckled. "That would have cost you a packet. Six or seven thousand riyals probably."

"This has been an expensive few weeks for you," Edward said as they left the courthouse.

"You don't need to tell me that," Peter replied.

*   *   *   *

Before Dick arrived on the scene, Mike Kelly was the most recent recruit to the Mottled team. Although he was new to the Arab world, Khajal was not his first experience of living abroad; after leaving university he had been an English teacher in Tours and Bordeaux for three years. Now just past his thirtieth birthday, his reasons for joining Monotone were largely financial; at the same time, he was not so naïve as to think that anyone could make a fortune by teaching English as a foreign language.

However, he was surprisingly naïve for his age in certain other respects and one result of this was that, not long after Peter's brush with the law, he found himself in what could have been quite serious trouble.

He was a pleasant, undemanding young man with an imposing presence (he was over six feet tall and heavily built), who made friends easily and was happy in his job, and he had a warm and trusting relationship with his Khajali pupils.

Shortly after Peter's Traffic Court case, he decided to buy a car so that he could get out more at the weekends and explore the local desert and beaches. Apart from some spectacular sand dunes in the south of the country, Khajal's terrain was generally flat, yellow-grey, stony, barren and rather dull, but Mike had discovered some fossilized bivalves and sea urchins several miles inland during a recent day trip with his trainees, and he had undergone an instant reincarnation as a dedicated fossil hunter. Nobody else had shown the slightest interest, so he realised that if he was to pursue his new passion in future he would need to rely on his own transport.

Although the fees Monotone charged Mottled Oil were quite high, most of the branch's income went on local administration and the monthly remittance to London rather than the teachers and Mike knew that he would not be able to afford a brand new car on his salary - particularly one capable of handling Khajal's rough terrain - so he asked his students if they could help him find a cheap but roadworthy secondhand four-wheel drive vehicle. A few days later Salim announced that a friend of his had an oldish Suzuki for sale and took Mike along to inspect it.

Mike knew how to drive, but anything technical was a complete mystery to him. He knew how to start the engine and make the car move forwards and backwards, but as far as he was concerned, problems like breakdowns and funny noises were beyond his ken and needed to be left to the experts. Fortunately, Mottled Oil had no shortage of technical experts and one of the older members of Mike's class was a trained motor mechanic, so he took him along with him to look at the Suzuki and recommend a price.

The verdict was positive. Mike's adviser concluded that the Suzuki still had a fair bit of life left in it and the two parties agreed on a price of 5,000 riyals.

The next problem was the driving licence. Mike had a UK licence which would have qualified him for a temporary Khajali licence if it had been valid, but it had expired, so this meant he would only be allowed to drive in Khajal if he signed up for lessons as a registered learner driver and passed the local driving test. This could take several months, particularly if he failed the test on the first and second attempts. He explained the problem to Salim.

"That's OK," Salim said. "I've got a friend in the vehicle licensing department who will probably be able to fix something. I'll ask him what details he needs and let you know."

Mike was relieved and delighted. Some days later he wrote in his journal:-

"Salim has come up trumps. From now on I'm going to call him Mr. Fixit. If there are ever any problems that need sorting out, he is the man to go to. First he managed to find me a cheapish car that works and now he has wangled me a Khajali driving licence. It cost me a bit more than I would have had to pay if I had gone through official channels, but at least I can drive now."

Three weeks later he wrote:-

"Disaster! Everything was going so well, too. It made an unimaginable difference having my own transport and this last weekend's fossil hunt was my best ever. I found two gigantic cone shells the size of door stoppers, a beautifully patterned sea urchin and a crab (no pincers but you could clearly see its eye sockets). You might think being alone in the desert is a bit frightening, and I'm sure it would be if you were stuck miles away from anywhere, particularly in the summer, but I always knew where I was, I was never very far from the main road and I had plenty of water.

"Dusk had fallen when I got to the outskirts of Khajal City on the way home, and that was when it happened. As I was driving along minding my own business I heard the siren of a police motor-cycle behind me and I realised that it was telling me to stop - which of course I did dutifully. A policeman dismounted and came up to me.

"'Did you realise your left rear light isn't working?' he asked. In quite a polite, friendly tone.

"'No,' I said. 'I'm sure it was OK when I set off.'

"'I suppose you realise you are committing an offence,' he said.

"'I do now,' I replied. 'I'm really sorry. I'll get it fixed as soon as I can find a garage.'

"'In the meantime, I'll have to see your licence and *mulkiyah*,' he said.

"I handed over my driving licence and the car's log book and he called up his office on his walkie-talkie. They had quite a long conversation which I couldn't understand and then the policeman signed off and turned to me.

"'There's a question about your licence,' he said. 'I see that the one I have here says Michael Kelly, but my colleague says the licence they have on record with this number is a defunct one that was issued to a Mubarak bin Rashid al Hajeri. I'm afraid you'll have to follow me to the police station so that we can sort it all out.'

"When we got to the police station the officer in charge looked at my licence and said it was a fake. Then he confiscated it along with my Suzuki and sent a constable with me in a police car so that I could collect my passport from my flat. Back at the station, they took down all my details and told me I would be hearing from them 'in the near future'.

"I thought this episode was just one of those tiresome and not very serious things that tend to happen in Khajal from time to time, but when Edward learnt about it he took a much less sanguine view.

"'I don't want to alarm you unnecessarily, but there could be major consequences. For a start, there is bound to be a court case,' he said. 'From what I understand from your account of it, it sounds as if you have been trying to pass off a forgery as a genuine article, and I don't expect the Khajalis will be at all happy about it. Still, for the moment there is really nothing either of us can do, so we'll just have to wait and see what happens.'"

For the next few weeks there was silence. Salim was apologetic and cursed his friend who had produced the phoney licence, and eventually he managed to retrieve Mike's Suzuki and sell it for him at a slight loss. Then one day a summons arrived from the Traffic Court.

"Oh hello. You again. I see you've got a new customer this time," the chubby Egyptian judge said to Edward as he entered the courtroom with Mike in tow. "I hope your visits here are not going to become a habit, though I realise that in both cases so far you are not the actual culprit." He picked up Mike's case file and opened it. "I've had a look at your friend's file and I'm sorry to say he is in real trouble. A forged driving licence is a serious crime, not a trivial matter."

"I can't tell you how sorry I am," Mike said. "I never realised the licence wasn't genuine."

"But you must have used improper means to get it. The authorities don't hand out fake licences to people who go through the proper channels." He turned to Edward. "What do you say, Mr. Manager?"

"I have spoken to him severely and he would like to offer his sincere apologies. All I can say in mitigation is that he is very new in this country and hasn't yet learnt the proper way of doing things," Edward said.

"I suppose you realise that the usual punishment for passing forged documents is a year's imprisonment followed by deportation?" the judge said.

Mike gasped and went pale.

"However, I appreciate that you were new to this country when you committed the offence, so I shall impose a lighter penalty. You must pay a fine of two and a half thousand riyals... All right. You may go now. Payment within seven days. Your boss will remember the payment procedure from last time."

"Blimey, that's more than a month's salary," Edward said as they headed back to the Mottled training centre. "What are you going to do about it? Can you lay your hands on the money within the next week?"

"Yes, thank God. I had to transfer nearly all my assets from England to buy the Suzuki, but now that Salim has sold it for me I've got most of it back so I'll be able to cover the fine... Though of course I'll be even worse off now than I was before I joined Monotone... Funny thing though... I don't really feel too upset about what's happened. I only came to Khajal because of the salary - that was what attracted me in the first place - but actually I'm growing rather fond of this country and as long as I can eat, have a decent social life and live reasonably comfortably, I think I'm going to enjoy living here. And I've made some good friends, particularly Salim. Even if he has cost me an arm and a leg, his heart's in the right place and he means well."

5.

A VISIT FROM THE BOSS

I t was one of those balmy March days. The land basked serenely under a sun that was so benign and gentle that those with very short memories might have been forgiven for thinking that Khajal was blessed with a perfect climate. The sporadic rains of the previous four months had given the desert a sparse scattering of pink, yellow and white flowers and straggly grey-green grass, while reviving the tired thorn bushes, acacias and creeping colocynth vines with their hard, bitter fruits like striped green tennis balls, and enticing the urban population out of the city to comb the scrubby ground for the popular spring delicacy *yarawa* - a kind of milkweed with soft prickles that an expat wag had famously described as a slimy miniature loofah dipped in treacle. Over in the west of the Khajal Peninsula herds of camels and their owners had arrived in the country from regions far afield over the border where the earth was still parched and grazing was scarce.

This was normally Edward's favourite time of year, but today the joys of spring left him cold and unmoved. As he looked glumly out of the window of his flat at the school car park, sipping a moody glass of tea, he felt surer than ever that it would soon be time to bid farewell to Monotone and Khajal and move on to pastures new. His had never been an adventurous spirit and, as usual, the prospect of change daunted him.

He was feeling out of sorts for two reasons. A couple of days earlier, the landlord of the teachers' villa had sent Nader, his agent, round with a letter announcing that he would be raising the monthly rent on the teachers' villa from a thousand to fifteen hundred riyals with immediate effect. This was technically illegal; soon after the 1970s oil boom started a new regulation had been announced in the *Khajal Gazette* banning rent rises of more than ten per cent every two years, but the landlord was from a rival branch of the ruling family and had little respect for the current government and its edicts. Meanwhile the Emir himself - who had recently come to power through a coup against his cousin and still feared the enmity of those who had clout and influence - generally raised no objection if his relatives chose to abuse the law in minor ways as long as they had no plans to unseat him.

"You can't do this," Edward said.

"Really? You think not?" said the agent, a scrawny, sour-faced man who considered himself an honorary member of the ruling family because he had been brought up as a slave in the former Emir's father's household. "Of course we can do this. We can do what we like. I could have you thrown out of the country if I wanted to."

"I'm not so sure about that," Edward said. "...Anyway, I'm only the local manager. I don't have the authority to suddenly start paying out that sort of money. I'll have a word with my boss in London and see what he says."

"That's your business. I don't care how you do it, but next month you'll give me one and a half thousand riyals. Otherwise... Out! And when I say out, I mean it!" With a harsh staccato laugh, the agent got into his Cadillac and drove off, throwing up a shower of dust and gravel as he swished out of the car park.

Monotone could actually afford to pay the extra rent without having to cut back drastically on other expenses, but "Sod this for a lark!" said Edward to himself. "As far as I'm concerned, the law's the law and I'm bloody well going to fight that arrogant bastard. Or at least string him along for a while with the fiction that I can't make my own decisions and need London's approval. Who the hell does he think he is?"

Edward's other worry was Freddy, his boss.

Freddy was due to arrive in Khajal at the beginning of May accompanied by the London auditor. His tour of the Gulf branches was an annual event - partly to check that his managers were not being over-generous with the staff or themselves but mainly to examine the branch bank accounts and siphon off anything that he decided was "surplus" (which usually meant emptying the local emergency funds), even if this meant that his "man on the spot" had to take a salary cut for a while. ("Sorry Edward/Richard/Oliver, but our need is greater than yours. We'll soon be raking it in of course but in the meantime Head Office in Kensington has got sky-high rents to pay... We all have to make sacrifices from time to time and in any case you are being paid more than the teachers.")

Although frugality was Monotone's guiding principle, a different set of rules applied to its proprietor and during his business trips Freddy always insisted on staying at the best hotels at the local branch's expense. Edward only discovered this after booking him and the auditor into the Orient Inn - a respectable but unpalatial establishment near the souq.

"What's the swimming pool like? Olympic-size?" Freddy asked when the arrangements for the visit were being finalised.

"It hasn't got a swimming pool but people who've stayed at the Orient tell me they like it. Mottled Oil usually put their new intermediate staff there for a few days if their permanent accommodation isn't ready... They all say it is excellent."

"Hmm... Intermediate staff... You mean Indian and Egyptian clerks and people like that... But Edward... How shall I put this? ... We don't want to lower the tone, do we? Monotone need to keep up their standards and it won't do our image any good if the boss comes out to the Gulf and is seen to be staying in a doss-house ... I suggest you put Maurice and me in the Khajal Palace Hotel. Or the new Grand."

So Freddy and auditor were booked into the Khajal Palace Hotel - a nearly-majestic edifice on the seafront which was marginally cheaper than the new Grand and had a swimming pool that might almost have passed for Olympic-sized to the untrained eye.

As expected, the agent returned at the end of March to collect the monthly rent. Edward handed him a cheque for a thousand riyals which he refused disdainfully.

"Didn't I make it clear to you that it is fifteen hundred riyals?" he said. "Not a thousand. One and a half thousand. Now."

"Sorry, I'm afraid you'll have to wait," Edward said. "My boss says he'll give me an answer in a week or two."

"I see. Then you must leave the property tomorrow. I told you before that you must get out if you don't pay up and you haven't paid up. If your things are still in the house at midday tomorrow my men and I will throw them into the street."

"Perhaps I have been a bit rash and allowed my bloody-mindedness to get the better of me. After all, it wouldn't have ruined Monotone if I had given in to him," Edward said to himself after Nader had left. He was almost sure the agent was bluffing, but he was now starting to experience an attack of distinctly cold feet so he went to the central police station to ask for protection. The Sudanese desk sergeant was sympathetic but said there was nothing he could do because the duty officer had already gone home.

"Come back tomorrow and tell him all about it," he said. "He's a Khajali so he may be able to help. It's quite clear that you are in the right, but foreigners in my position can't do anything when there are Khajalis involved, especially if they are members of the Family... Even though we are the police."

Fearing that the agent might decide not to wait till the morrow and opt instead for a raid in the small hours, Edward spent a sleepless night in the villa with its two resident teachers - Roy Sladen and Mike Kelly. In such a situation, most normal people would generally resent being on the front line in someone else's battle and in this respect Roy and Mike were no exceptions. Normally the most placid and easy-going of Edward's colleagues, they were both furious with him for putting their home in jeopardy and that evening they made it emphatically clear to him. ("It's just pig-headedness on your part. Nothing more than that. And it's us, not you, who are being made the sacrificial lambs, so now you can bloody well hold the fort for us and let us get some sleep. *Some* of us have to go to work tomorrow.")

Edward returned to the police station at seven o'clock the next morning after an anxious but uneventful night. The duty officer, a young Khajali lieutenant called Saif al Ka'bi, whose shift had just begun, listened to the story and drove round to the property with him and a constable.

"Is that your car?" the lieutenant said, pointing to a Cadillac parked outside the front gate.

"No. It looks like the agent's."

"Seems we have arrived just in time then." He got out of the patrol car.

"Hello," he called. "Anyone at home?"

They heard the sound of a heavy drum scraping on concrete, then the clunk of a drum being upended and the agent's head popped up over the garden wall. He looked a little taken aback at the sight of the police but decided to brazen it out.

"Oh! Good morning officer. Just checking the property," he said. "The tenants haven't been looking after it and they've allowed it to get into a terrible state... Talk about mess! You should see it. Leaves and dust everywhere. It can't have been swept for months! And one of the windows looks like it's going to fall off its hinges."

"How did you get in?"

"Over the wall. The key didn't fit. They must have changed the lock."

"Who gave you permission?"

"I've just told you. I was checking the property."

"Did the tenants say you could enter it when they were out?"

"Call my employer. He will confirm that I'm here with his approval..."

"That's not what I asked. If the tenants didn't give you permission you are breaking the law."

"But my employer told me to go in. Check with him. He's Sheikh..."

"I know perfectly well who he is... Listen... You are not above the law and neither is he. You'll have to come with us to the police station."

"OK. If you say so. I'll follow you in my car."

"No you won't. You're coming with us."

"What about my car?"

"Give us the keys and we'll take care of it."

Scowling, the agent climbed reluctantly into the back of the patrol car, ushered by the constable, and Edward rode in front with the lieutenant.

"Well that's all settled then," said Lieutenant al Ka'bi back at the police station. "You shouldn't have anything more to worry about from now on... We'll hold Nader for a day or two and make him sign an undertaking not to bother you and we'll tell his boss to deal with you in a strictly legal way from now on. I don't care whether he is a Sheikh or not. Any more trouble from either of them and you let me know immediately."

Back at the school, Edward called Mottled Oil and told Roy and Mike that the problem had been resolved.

At eight o'clock that evening he had a call from Roy at the villa.

"The landlady's just been round here and she made a terrible scene. Apparently it's her house, not her husband's though everybody thinks it's his, and - from what she was saying... I couldn't catch much, she was screeching like a fishwife... but I gather she thinks we've kidnapped her agent. She left a few minutes ago but she says she will be back very soon with reinforcements. You'd better come round and speak to her."

"OK. I'll be with you in a few minutes."

All was quiet at the villa when Edward arrived, but at half past eight there was the sound of a heavy vehicle drawing up outside followed by a deafening drum roll on the iron gate. When Edward opened it he was met by a torrent of abuse from a small elderly woman wearing the traditional black cloak and female face mask. She was flanked by two sheepish Indian attendants who looked as if they were trying to blend into the background.

"You! You! You are thieves and robbers! Give me my agent!" she screamed. "What have you done with him? We sent him round here this morning and nobody has seen him all day. What have you done with him? Did you kill him? You've killed him, haven't you?"

"He's been arrested and now he's at the police station," Edward explained.

"You're lying! Why should anyone arrest him?"

"He broke the law. He broke into the house without permission."

"*Ma fi qanun*! (There is no law!) *Ana bi nafsi qanun*! (I myself am the law!). I've got just as much authority as the Emir, may Allah curse him. The police can't do anything to us."

Edward exchanged glances with one of the attendants and gave him a half smile.

"Huh! So now you're making fun of me, are you? Stop mocking

me! This is my country! If you want to mock, go and mock in your own country. I'll have you thrown out of Khajal! Huh! How dare you sneer like that?"

"I'm sorry. I wish I could help you, but I'm afraid I can't," Edward said with as straight a face as he could manage. "If you want your agent, you'd better talk to the police."

She departed with her retinue, muttering angry oaths.

A few days later, Nader came round to the school looking slightly (but not very) chastened and accepted a cheque for a thousand riyals.

Edward's next problem was how to handle Freddy. He had only met him briefly a few times and most of his information about him was based on hearsay from second- and third-hand sources, but Steve Kettle was able to brief him because he had actually worked with him for a few months (a period he referred to as "Monotone Mark One") soon after Freddy had set up his first language school in one of the other Gulf states.

"He is likeable, amusing and intelligent but you have to handle him with extreme caution and take everything he says with more than a pinch of salt," Steve told him. "Slippery is probably the politest word to describe him, though it could be a bit of an understatement. I remember back in those days he and his wife Lucinda made a formidable team and they always had a number of cunning ploys up their sleeves for getting out of scrapes."

"Like what?"

"For example, he had an emergency button concealed under his desk and if he had an awkward situation... you know, like a pushy creditor, rows over pay or holiday arrangements, or perhaps an angry staff member threatening to complain about him to the Ministry of Labour... he would press the button and Lucinda would appear and tell him he was urgently required elsewhere. It could be really infuriating if you had something you seriously needed to talk to him about because you would find yourself being casually dismissed as if you had just called in for a friendly chat:

"'Good of you to drop by, Steve. Thanks for coming. I'll have to go now and find out what this fellow wants, but we must talk again soon. It's been great to see you, as always.'

"Once, I remember... it was three days after pay day and I still hadn't received my salary so I went to see him and found Lucinda with him in the office. I thought I had him cornered as he couldn't very well summon her with his emergency button, but the two of them were able to wriggle out of it and make me feel like a heartless brute at the same time:

"'Hmm... You want some money do you Steve? What, now? Let me see... I don't think I have any on me at the moment. Have you got any money darling?'

"'One minute Freddy. I'll just get my bag... Yes. I've got half a dinar... Oh, and two hundred fils... You take it Steve... That's all right. I'm sure you need it, and the children will be able to manage without milk on their cornflakes tomorrow morning.'

"'No. That's OK Lucinda. I don't want you to go short. Of course your children must have milk on their cornflakes.'

"'No, no. Please, I insist. I'm sure your need is greater than ours. Take it.'"

("Freddy: 'Yes, do take it Steve.'")

"In the end I pocketed the half dinar but I felt that I was... Well, you know. I realised it was all a game but they made me feel I was the one doing them down rather than the other way round."

"Another thing about Freddy is that he suddenly gets these wild enthusiasms which he tends to drop just as quickly - before they've had a chance to bear fruit but not before he has wasted a lot of money on them... Some of them, of course, he should never have even dreamt of starting in the first place. You remember his mad scheme to set up secretarial institutes for local girls in Saudi

Arabia and Yemen which never got off the ground! Well, that was nowhere near being his daftest... Shortly before I stopped working for him - that's to say, near the end of Monotone Mark One - he had the bright idea of opening a samosa restaurant."

"And giving up language teaching?"

"No. The school was doing rather well. In fact, it might have made sense if he had just opened a little samosa, sandwich and soft drinks kiosk for the students in their reception area but he had bigger ideas...

"The whole thing started when Safiyyah, the school's Pakistani receptionist, invited him and Lucinda to dinner at her house. Safiyyah's mother, who is a marvellous cook, served them some unusual home-made samosas with various fillings that she had invented herself and Freddy was bowled over. So bowled over, in fact, that he seriously suggested on the spot that they should go into business together. Lucinda and Safiyyah were a bit sceptical, but the mother thought it was quite an intriguing idea so it was agreed in principle that they would open a place in town; she would do the cooking and Freddy would provide the commercial expertise. There would be fifty-seven-plus varieties of samosas - some sweet and some savoury; the fillings would include prawns, duck and ginger, mussels, crab... Christmas mince pie mix, lamb and mint sauce... cheese and onion, cheese without onion, broad beans and coriander, marmalade, strawberry jam, banana etc. as well as the traditional curried vegetable and spicy mincemeat versions. Freddy was convinced he was onto a winner and a few days later he signed a very expensive lease for a vacant restaurant he had spotted by chance when he was driving around in a posh part of town. Without doing a feasibility study or anything.

"Of course that would never have happened if he had bothered to sit down first and think for a few minutes about costs. Everybody knows that samosas are about the cheapest street snack imaginable and the standard versions are available all over the Gulf, but Freddy was convinced that the public would come flocking to buy his superior gourmet products at gourmet prices..."

"So what happened?"

"Fortunately, Lucinda intervened so the idea was scrapped before they got as far as buying chairs and tables or equipment or taking out a commercial licence. Even so, getting out of the restaurant lease proved very costly."

Khajal was Freddy's second port of call on his tour of the Gulf and Edward met him and Maurice, the auditor, at the airport after a half-hour flight from the neighbouring state where Monotone also had a branch.

"An odd-looking pair," thought Edward, as they emerged from the customs tunnel into the arrivals hall. "I don't know why - I was expecting Maurice to be a low key version of Freddy but these two are more like Laurel and Hardy... though a well-groomed Laurel and a deluxe edition of Hardy... Freddy - slim, fit and elegant... and Maurice - fat, pale, sweaty and pampered, Gucci shirt straining at the buttons, stomach hanging out over his belt and a bulging leather briefcase."

"Would you like a rest before we get down to business?" Edward asked when he had checked them into their hotel.

No, they assured him. They were feeling fresh, full of pep and raring to go.

"And by the way, congratulations on your victory over that agent. You showed plenty of initiative there. I can see you've got the Monotone nose for saving money," Freddy said.

"Thanks," said Edward, blushing modestly. "It was a pleasant surprise considering that I was up against a member of the ruling family."

"Yes. I was wondering about that. Normally one might expect the dice to be loaded against you. In fact, it could have been you spending a night in the cells for complaining about someone with such powerful connections."

"Actually, I wasn't too worried," Edward said. "Everyone knows that the Ruler is thoroughly fed up with that branch of the family and, according to my Khajali sources, nothing could please him more than to have an excuse to put them in their place. Though of course... if it had been the Sheikh himself or his wife, and not the agent, who broke into our house, I don't think anyone would have been arrested and the police would probably have advised me to agree to their terms."

The first thing Freddy wanted to do was call on the customers - that is to say, George Weever at Mottled Oil and, time permitting, Major Rashid, the commander of the army training centre where Monotone supplied an English teacher for the new batches of officer cadets. Where Mottled were concerned, some smoothing of ruffled feathers was required. Memories of the previous year's Jim Barrett disaster were still raw in Weever's mind (and the year before that there had also been one or two somewhat less spectacular blunders), and Edward suggested a humble apology from the big boss - or at least a show of contrition - might be a good tactical move.

"OK. Though our first priority must be to persuade them to put up our fees," Freddy said. Maurice agreed. "We're too cheap and that's why our teachers aren't given the same respect and privileges as most of the other Western subcontractors... I'm sure Mottled's subconscious attitude is 'We're paying peanuts so we're getting monkeys, and monkeys can't be allowed access to our senior staff facilities'. Of course they could never say that openly. Look... they could afford to pay us five times, ten times, our present fee and it wouldn't make the slightest difference to them financially... And if they pay us more we could even pass a bit of it on to our staff if they start playing up. And in fact" (for Freddy this was really quite a new and revolutionary idea) "we could even advertise higher salaries for our new recruits and try to get better qualified and more competent people."

"The increase will have to be across the board," Maurice said. "If Mottled get to hear that they are being charged more and the army isn't, they will say they're being taken for a ride because they're a rich oil company."

"Yes, I understand that," Edward said. "But we can't charge them both an identical rate because the terms of our contracts with Mottled and the army are not the same. The hours are different and the duties are different, and in any case the army training centre's budget is controlled by the Defence Ministry so we can't negotiate fees with them. They decide what we will be paid. And Richard, their teacher, lives in army accommodation near the *Qala'ah* so we don't build his housing into our costs."

"So the only thing we can discuss with Major Rashid is the training programme and whether they would like us to supply any additional teachers?"

"More or less. Yes."

George Weever had been warned of Freddy's imminent arrival and arranged to meet him and Edward after lunch. Meanwhile, Maurice would spend the afternoon in Edward's office going through the branch's books.

Weever received Edward with his standard bluff, genial, being-friendly-to-underlings-and-subcontract-employees-past-and-present manner. Freddy's welcome was noticeably cooler, even verging on the austere; however, he had plenty of experience of brush-offs and worse from disgruntled customers so he was unfazed and, after apologising fulsomely for the Barrett disaster (and several less spectacular earlier cock-ups), he suggested that what Mottled Oil really needed was more English teachers.

"Edward tells me you are expanding your training programmes

and of course we are more than ready to do our bit. Just give the word."

"No, we won't be running any additional language classes. It's true we are expanding; naturally we want to employ more Cadgerlies with the skills the oil industry needs, but that means technical programmes. We'll be bringing out new instructors, but they'll be giving technical training to mechanics, electricians, assistant drillers... people like that."

"I expect Monotone could help you there as well," Freddy said.

"I very much doubt if you could. Unless I'm greatly mistaken, you haven't any expertise in those fields... and in any case we already have plenty of our own in-house training staff who, I can assure you, are highly competent and extremely well qualified."

Then the discussion turned to costs. Over his years in the Gulf, Freddy had sharpened his bargaining skills and in situations like these he was in his element. Weever, on the other hand, was a relative novice. For most of his pre-Khajal career he had been an office bureaucrat in London, Oslo and The Hague. Haggling was alien to his nature and during his occasional forays into the local souq he left any wrangling over the prices of handicrafts and trinkets to Mrs. Weever. When negotiating over fees for Mottled Oil's contractors he was normally supported by Abu Musa, the Palestinian Assistant Finance Manager, whose haggling skills were legendary, but Abu Musa was on holiday in Jordan so Weever was on his own.

The negotiation was conducted in three phases. First, Freddy said how happy he was to be working with Mottled, but that the oil-boom had brought inflation and "we are finding it difficult to make ends meet, as I'm sure you will appreciate". Weever conceded that prices had gone up, but added: "You can hardly deny that what we are paying you is already very generous".

"In the past - that's to say, three or four years ago - it was certainly, well, adequate," Freddy said. "But I'm afraid it is nowhere near enough today."

This was the start of phase two.

"What sort of figure are you thinking of?" Weever asked.

"Well, you are paying us five thousand riyals a month per teacher at the moment and with the huge rises in rents and other costs we can't really make any kind of profit with less than eight and a half thousand." Freddy was aiming at about six and a half thousand, but he would have been ready to accept anything over five thousand eight hundred.

"Wheeeuw", Weever whistled. "That's a bit steep."

Freddy produced a list of costings which he and Lucinda had concocted before he left London. These were based on some background information from Edward and a dollop of fact-free imaginative input inspired by his experience of living in the Gulf during the previous decade. Weever had little idea about the cost of living outside the confines of Mottled Oil, and so without the support of Abu Musa he was unable to rebut or counter Freddy's figures with anything substantial of his own. Even so, he felt that an increase of over sixty per cent would be hard to justify to his bosses, so he grabbed a figure out of the air.

"We might be able to manage six thousand," he said.

Phase three, which followed, was brief and to the point.

"Seven," Freddy said. "I think we could probably squeeze by on seven at a pinch."

"I can offer you six and a half. That's the most I can do."

"Oh no. I don't think we can... Just a minute... That's cutting it tight... but, okay." Freddy sighed with a look of resignation on his handsome face. "It looks like you're not going to move any further so let's agree on six and a half. You drive a hard bargain." Weever smiled smugly.

"You see, that's the way to do it," said Freddy as they headed back to the Monotone branch office. "Let them think they've fought a tough battle and won. Now let's see what Maurice has to say about the way you've been handling the finances."

As it turned out, Maurice had nothing to say. When they entered the office they found him lying on his back on the floor with his eyes open, staring sightlessly at the ceiling. The executive swivel chair he had been sitting on lay on its side next to him.

"He's clearly dead," said Freddy briskly after checking Maurice's pulse and breathing and finding them both absent. "I think we'd better call the police and see if we can rustle up an ambulance to take him away... As far as I remember that was the procedure when Robin Walters dropped dead in the classroom a few years ago. That was before your time of course and in one of our other branches... Are you all right Edward? You look as if you could do with an ambulance yourself."

6.

FOILED AGAIN

"I know this is all a bit of a shock, but that's no reason to go to pieces," said Freddy. He looked reproachfully at Edward who was white and trembling, his mouth quivering and a blank, frozen expression on his face. They were sitting on classroom chairs by the school entrance waiting for the police and ambulance to arrive while Maurice - the corporeal part of him - was lying where they had found him on the floor of the office. Although they knew he was dead they had toyed briefly with the idea of trying to bring him back to life with mouth-to-mouth resuscitation but, when they realised that that he had already started to cool down and it would be pointless as well as unpleasant, they closed his eyes and covered him with a sheet from Edward's flat.

"What time dot he first classes start?"

"Four o'clock."

"You'd better stick a notice on the door saying that the school is closed today due to unforeseen circumstances. And get Hussain - is that his name? - or the other cleaner to stand at the entrance and make sure the students get the message. There'll be police and God knows who else tramping all over the place in a few minutes... They seem to be taking their time, don't they? It must be nearly half an hour since you called them."

"Well I can assure you, I did call them. You heard me. And the ambulance people... I wonder what actually happened. With Maurice, I mean," Edward said.

"Heart attack. At least, that would be my guess. He looked pretty unhealthy, didn't he? More or less a classic case I should imagine. In his fifties, drank too much, smoked too much, ate too much rich food, took no exercise to speak of... That's a recipe for clogged arteries, high blood pressure and... you know. There are loads of Western expatriates like that in this part of the world and the Christian cemeteries up and down the Gulf are full of them...

"Anyway... people like you and me don't have to worry about that sort of thing," he concluded smugly, patting his slim stomach. "I take plenty of exercise and you look pretty fit too."

He peered into the entrance hall and wrinkled his nose.

"Incidentally, you really must do something about the décor here in the school. It's tawdry and depressing as well as antiquated in the extreme. Did you inherit it from your predecessor?"

"Oh. I always thought it looked rather nice. Cosy and welcoming... One of our students said that when he came here he felt he was entering a little bit of England in a foreign land."

"Well, he must have been off his head, or perhaps he was just being polite... or practising a new English expression. Just look at all those dreary tourist board posters of guardsmen in bearskin hats... London buses, Big Ben and the Houses of Parliament... red telephone boxes... Carnaby Street... Honestly, Carnaby Street? I ask you! How passé is that? All stuck on to the walls with lumps of Blu-Tack? Half of them aren't even straight! Even I can see that and I haven't got a very good eye... And those ancient copies of *Modern English* and the other tatty magazines in the students' tea and coffee area! They must be as old as this building. Older probably..."

He was about to add that the classrooms could also do with a lick of paint when he was interrupted by the arrival of a police car. A cross-looking uniformed sergeant disembarked accompanied by a constable and a small plainclothes detective in Khajali dress.

"Who's in charge here? Where's the body?" the sergeant barked. As Edward was about to show them upstairs to the office the ambulance arrived and a couple of men unloaded a stretcher from the patient compartment.

"You'll have to wait," the sergeant told them. "We've just arrived ourselves and we haven't seen the corpse yet or taken down any details. Is one of you a doctor?"

"No, we're just ambulance men. We take patients to the hospital and if they're dead the pathologist examines them in the path. lab."

Edward ushered the police into the office. "Do you need me here?" he asked.

"Yes. You'd better stay in case we want to ask some questions, but keep out of our way. We don't want you cluttering up the place."

The sergeant removed the sheet and the detective turned the body over after taking a few Polaroid photographs of the scene.

"There seems to be some blood on the back of his head," he said to the sergeant. "Look. His hair is matted."

"Hmm. Not heart attack or stroke then. Murder most probably," the sergeant said. "Where were you when this happened?" he demanded, fixing Edward with an accusing stare.

"My boss and I were at the Mottled Oil offices all afternoon and we only got back here less than an hour ago... When we left this man he seemed perfectly OK. He and my boss have only been in this country a few hours. He's never been here before so I can't see why anyone could possibly want to murder him."

"We'll have to see what the pathologist says. What was he doing in this country anyway?"

"He and my boss - the man you met downstairs - are touring the Gulf to visit our company's branches. This man - this late man - is an auditor and he was checking our accounts."

"Aha... So *if* he was murdered it could have something to do with money. Maybe he was about to discover evidence of embezzlement or misuse of funds? Have you got any witnesses to confirm that you were where you say you were this afternoon?"

"Of course I have. Apart from my boss, there is the Mottled Oil Personnel Manager and several of his office staff."

"Was the school empty during that time apart from the deceased?"

"Apart from the two cleaners, but they only arrived shortly before we did. They didn't see anything and when we got back they hadn't started cleaning the office so they didn't know the man was dead."

The detective decided he had seen all he needed to see for the time being and the sergeant gave the ambulance men permission to take the body to the hospital.

"We can definitely discount murder. I've never heard such a ridiculous suggestion," Freddy said after the police had left. "Though it's odd that there was dried blood on the back of his head. He must have fallen very heavily. Perhaps he was tilting back in his chair and it overbalanced, tipped him onto the floor and he fractured his skull. That could certainly have lethal consequences I should imagine."

*　　*　　*　　*

News of Maurice's demise had the Khajali grapevine working overtime and by the next morning the teachers at the Mottled

Oil Training Centre were in great demand as potential sources of juicy details. The trainees were a little disappointed that the reality appeared to be more prosaic than the rumour machine had suggested.

"It's all right," Tech 2a insisted when they suspected Roy Sladen knew a lot more than he was prepared to admit. "You can trust us. We're not blabbermouths. Not a word you say will go beyond these four walls if you don't want it to. Now tell us what really happened. Was he stabbed or shot? ... Do they know who did it?"

"I haven't been into the school since it happened and all I know is what I've heard from Edward, which isn't very much," Roy told them. "But I understand he was definitely not stabbed or shot and probably died from natural causes, though the police are still keeping an open mind."

The class muttered sceptically.

Curiosity about "this Maurice business" (as Freddy had euphemistically described it) was not solely the preserve of the trainees and staff at the training centre. Later that morning, Edward had a call from George Weever.

"We at Mottled need to know what's going on. There are so many rumours floating around," he said. "Perhaps I could have a word with your boss."

"Not possible I'm afraid. He left for Dubai at the crack of dawn this morning because he said he had other branches to visit and wanted to get out of Khajal quickly to avoid getting caught up in any investigation. Not that the police seriously suspect him or anything, but if there are question marks over the death there might be complications and I suppose they could stop any potential witnesses from leaving the country. And after all, we were the ones who found the body."

"I see. So he's left you holding the baby so to speak."

"Yes... Though I'm sure that's not how he would put it."

"What do you mean by question marks over the death? He was

definitely murdered, wasn't he? I've been hearing he was stabbed."

"Yes I've heard that too, but I can tell you for certain that that's nonsense. There were no stab wounds. He probably died of a heart attack, though they found some blood on the back of his head. Freddy and I suspect he fell backwards in his chair and maybe fractured his skull."

"So it looks an accident then?"

"Or natural causes. That's what we think."

*　　*　　*　　*

Over the next few days life returned to a semblance of normality, though Edward and the cleaners were gripped by heebie-jeebies whenever they went near the office and he moved most of the school's administrative paperwork to his flat. The police had taken a brief statement from him and Freddy when they came to view the body, and two days after "the incident" he had to call in at the central police station for a more formal interview. Freddy's absence was "not appreciated", the officer in charge told him, though it was not regarded as suspicious.

"Now let's hope that's the end of the matter as far as the police are concerned," Edward told his staff and colleagues.

However, a couple of weeks later he was summoned back to the police station.

"The report from the hospital has just come in and it says death was due to a brain haemorrhage following a heavy blow to the back of the head," the investigating officer told him.

"Well, he was a heavy man, so when he fell he would have fallen heavily. That would explain the heavy blow, wouldn't it?"

"The pathologist thinks he could have been hit with a blunt instrument."

"Could have been? But he probably wasn't?"

"He almost certainly was. In fact, we can say he certainly was. If his injury was caused by falling onto the tiled floor, there would probably have been no visible signs of trauma and no blood. However, his skin was broken and there was a noticeable indentation in his skull, which would suggest he was hit with something like a hammer."

"If that's true, I really can't understand it," Edward said. "My boss and I were nowhere near the place, the cleaners certainly didn't do it, because they had no motive and they would have arrived together... and in any case they were each aware of what the other was doing. They certainly wouldn't have conspired together to do something like that. You can discount that possibility one hundred per cent."

"Perhaps it was a burglar?"

"Why? Nothing was taken, and anyway there isn't anything worth stealing. A few school books and visual aids? A couple of old tape recorders? No. Definitely not."

Next, after the police had returned to the school and searched the building and garden for a weapon and found nothing, they questioned the teachers to eliminate them from their enquiries. This was regarded as rather a waste of time because the Mottled Oil teachers were at the Company's Training Centre and the army teacher was in his classroom at the Fort.

"Were all your teachers at the training centre all the time?" the investigating officer asked Roy.

"Yes. I'm pretty sure they were."

"Were they all teaching lessons all the afternoon?"

"Not all of them. One or two would have had a free lesson, in which case they would have spent it in the teachers' room."

Further inquiries revealed that Peter Frazer had actually been absent from the building for nearly an hour during the period in question because he had "some personal business" to attend to.

Pressed to explain what it was, he reluctantly admitted that he was having a surreptitious cup of tea in town with Salma, an Egyptian friend, while her parents were out for the afternoon.

"We may need to confirm this with her, but don't worry. We'll be discreet," the investigating officer told him. "Perhaps you could help us here Mr. Edward. Do you know her?"

"Yes. She had a temporary job at Mottled Oil last year when she was between school and college. I believe Peter actually wants to marry her, but he is afraid to ask her family."

"I can understand that. A Muslim girl and a Christian man. Marriage between them is not allowed. Or is she a Copt?"

"No, she's a Muslim but Peter says he would be ready to embrace Islam. The main problem is that her father is a top consultant at the hospital and Peter says he wants something better for his daughter than a simple English teacher with no prospects. Anyway, I can vouch for him. He's a good man and he couldn't possibly be involved in anything criminal, let alone murder."

At this point the investigations seemed to have reached a dead end and though it was assumed the police were still keeping their files open, Edward felt he and Monotone were now off the hook. He continued to run the branch with his usual style of ad-lib management (which he preferred to think of as refreshingly spontaneous), while at the same time continuing to hope for a change in his personal circumstances that would enable him to make a final escape to a less stressful job with another employer.

The classrooms were given a lick of cheap paint and the Blu-Tacked posters were replaced with Constable reproductions of the Haywain, Flatford Mill and Dedham Vale as well as scenes of the Lake District, Brighton Pier, Dover Castle, Birmingham's Spaghetti Junction, the Norfolk Broads, a half-ruined Cornish tin mine and various other inspiring locations. Some old *National Geographics* and *Sunday Times* colour supplements were added to the mouldering magazines on the tables in the tea and coffee area.

"I'd like to help you find another job but the trouble is you haven't really got much to offer apart from English teaching," said Salim - Edward's long-standing friend and former student. "With the present oil boom there's plenty of demand these days for engineers, electricians, architects, accountants, lawyers... loads of positions in fact - but you haven't got any technical qualifications or professional experience... or if you have you've kept very quiet about it. You're not even a good liar."

"I thought I was good at being devious."

"Well, you're not. If you were you could probably bluff your way into a well-paid job and survive in it for years without anyone rumbling you. There are hundreds of people like that in this country. Most of us suspect half the British management at Mottled Oil were street sweepers in their own country before they came out here and had everyone kowtowing to them."

"That's a bit of an exaggeration, but there may be a grain of truth in what you're saying. I'm told on good authority that the great Dr. Lewis, the Principal of the Khajal College of Business Administration Sciences, was plain primary school teacher Mr. Lewis back in England. Apparently he suddenly acquired a Ph.D. on the plane between London and Khajal and... well, look at him now. One of the leading lights of the local British community."

Shortly after the above conversation Salim told Edward that he had heard the newly opened Gulf States' Technical College was about to start looking for English teachers.

"It's a UN project and its students will be from nearly all the Gulf states, not just Khajal. The director of administration there is my cousin, and I know he will be happy to talk to you about it if you are interested."

"I certainly am! That sounds quite promising."

"OK. Let's see if we can meet him for a cup of coffee this

evening and have a word with him."

According to Salim's cousin, the College's new UN-appointed course directors had just discovered that their Khajali student intake were going to need an intensive English course. This had come as a huge surprise because they had been assured by the local UN office and the government that all the candidates had finished secondary school and spoke English fluently, and it was only after they had been assessed that it was discovered this was far from being the case.

"We have to accept them if the Ministry of Manpower sends them to us. The project has asked for secondary certificate holders and that's what they are... and if we say they're not good enough we'll be accused of slagging off our Khajali public education system which, as you know, claims to be among the best in the world... according to our government yearbook anyway," the cousin explained. "Come and talk to Bob, our project manager. He'll be able to explain things better than I can."

Bob Board was a genial middle-aged Australian who been with the UN for several years and had worked on training projects in Africa and South America. Khajal was his first Middle East posting.

"I've only been here five weeks and I'm still finding my feet," he told Edward. "Things aren't too easy at the moment. No problems with the local people of course and there's a lot of goodwill, but even so... And this latest hitch has come as a bit of a shock, to put it mildly. We've had pre-tech programmes in a lot of the other countries where I've worked and we're used to running our own English courses, but we were assured that the students here would be good enough to start their technical training right away."

"And they're really that weak in English?"

"Nearly all the Khajalis seem to be, though our assessment tests have shown that several of the non-Khajali candidates from the other Gulf states are pretty good. Good enough to go straight into a technical course anyway. Our main problem here is that our hands are tied. In most other places I've worked the projects aren't funded locally. The money is provided through our UN agency - the ILO. But this college is ninety per cent paid for by Khajal so we can't make policy decisions off our own bat and we're more or less at their beck and call... Anyway, the long and short of it is that we're going to need English teachers. And fast. The first batch of students are due to start in a few weeks."

"I'm sure our people in London would be able to send you some teachers. We could recruit them and fly them out... but... what about... erm... things like accommodation for instance? If they are going to be our employees, would you house them or would we? We'd need to know that before anything else because rented property is in very short supply here at the moment and it's getting more expensive by the day... And what about the syllabus? Would we use our own course material or would we be teaching yours?"

"Whoa! Hang on a minute... We haven't got the official go-ahead yet. At this stage all I can say is that if I was making the decisions I'd expect you people to take charge of the whole English programme and we would pay you a flat monthly fee... but so far we've only just started dropping broad hints to the Khajali government and we haven't approached the local language institutes yet. Apart from you, that is, and this is just an informal chat."

*   *   *   *

During his next meeting with the Minister of Manpower Bob explained the situation frankly to him, while tactfully avoiding any suggestion that Khajal's education system was not as good as the yearbook claimed, and it was agreed - provisionally - that Monotone should be asked to teach English to three classes of fifteen students for five hours a day.

"I'm not too happy about dealing with an independent company that isn't controlled either by us or by you though I appreciate this is an emergency and something has got to be done quickly," the Minister told Bob. "But don't involve me in any negotiations with the institute. Have a word with them about our proposal first and then let me know what they say."

Eventually it was agreed that Monotone would be asked to recruit three new teachers, fly them out from London and pay their salaries. It would receive a slightly higher fee than it was charging the army and the accommodation would be provided by the Khajali government. The situation would be reviewed after six months.

"And," the Minister told Bob, "we must have the final word on them. When the candidates have been identified let us have copies of their application forms and CVs. And photos. I want to see what they look like. Although Monotone is the only serious language institute in town, they can be amazingly incompetent sometimes. You are new to this country so you probably haven't heard about their disasters with Mottled Oil, but you will eventually, I'm sure."

Freddy was delighted with the latest developments. "Though make sure you get the agreement signed and stamped quickly before they can change their minds," he said.

"They wouldn't do that," Edward protested. "Everything has been agreed and Bob Board has given me his word."

"Nothing is agreed until everything is agreed in black and white and in writing," said Freddy. "You should know that by now. You've lived in Khajal long enough."

His caution was justified. When Edward went to sign the contract a few days later, Bob told him there had been a change of plan.

"Sorry. Please don't blame me. I'm as pissed off about this as you no doubt are," he said. "The Minister has decided that he wants the teachers to be employed directly by the Khajali government, not Monotone. He says they are willing to pay Monotone a generous recruitment fee but nothing more."

"Oh well," said Edward. "Win some, lose some."

"Anyway, what about you yourself? How would you like to join us?"

"Me, join you? What do you mean?"

"What I said. How would you fancy working for us?"

"You're actually offering me a job?"

"Well not exactly. I can't really do that because it is not in my hands, though if you are interested I could start the ball rolling."

"But you don't know anything about me."

"True. I don't, but I've heard via our admin. director that you might like a move from your present position and I gather his cousin's been singing your praises. Apparently your reputation as a teacher is second to none."

"That would be Salim, my old student. I wish he wouldn't do things like that. It's quite true... I'm not very happy in my present situation but I told him in confidence and I don't want everyone talking about it... and by the way, I certainly wouldn't describe myself as second to none. As a teacher I mean. Still, it was very kind of him to put in a good word for me."

"So you would like a move from Monotone?"

"Well, yes actually, but I can't just leave my present job. My boss would go through the roof."

"Would he be able to do anything to stop you legally? When does your contract with them finish?"

"I can't remember exactly. In about six or seven months I think. And it looks like you will be needing your new teachers within a couple of months. Or maybe sooner than that. I'm not saying I'm irreplaceable or anything but if I left Monotone as soon as that, our Khajal branch would be in a terrible mess."

"I think we can fix something with your employers. They're going to recruit three teachers for us (including you, assuming you join us), which would net them a substantial fee. And on top of that we would compensate them for having poached you... and of course pay them the cost of an air ticket for whoever flies out to replace you. I imagine one of your present colleagues could take over as branch manager and Monotone could send out another teacher to take his place. Or they could fly a new manager out from London."

"OK. I'd be happy to join you... if you'll have me and my present boss doesn't kick up too much of a fuss."

Fearing that Bob's offer might be too good to be true, for the next three weeks Edward tried to put his career plans at the back of his mind. From time to time Bob rang him to assure him that things were proceeding satisfactorily and he should be hearing some good news very soon. The college administration was happy with his CV and qualifications and the only remaining obstacle - if such it could be called - was the approval of the Minister's office which, he said, was "merely routine".

One evening there was a call from London.

"Edward, what's all this nonsense I hear about you planning to leave us?" Freddy demanded.

"Planning to leave you? I don't know what you mean."

"I was talking to George Weever on the phone today – he called me out of the blue because his daughter wants some information about language teaching as a career; anyway, he said he had heard you were applying for a job with that college we've been asked to recruit for. He said he'd heard it from Roy Sladen, who had been told by one of his trainees who had heard it from a friend of his."

"I might have said something vaguely to someone about a possible change of job sometime in the future, but that's all."

"If you were thinking of anything like that you should have discussed it with me. I'm prepared to put up with a lot of things but one thing I can't stand is disloyalty. Or treachery, to put it bluntly."

"Now please don't take it that way. Nothing's actually happening and it was just an idea."

"Well, if you ever think of doing something like that I would appreciate it if you'd let me know first rather than going behind my back. As a matter of courtesy if nothing else."

"Of course, Freddy."

Steve Kettle, the only teacher in Khajal to have worked for Monotone twice, told Edward not to worry.

"Freddy never has a good word to say about anyone who leaves him after discovering that the grass is greener elsewhere," he said. "To hear him talk about them you'd think they were a waste of space and he is glad to be rid of them, even when they go on to have distinguished careers elsewhere... Looking at our lot, you might find that hard to believe but it does happen sometimes. Olly Howard - one of my old colleagues from way back - is a linguistics professor at some university in Wales now and he used to teach basic English to middle-aged tugmen on one of Monotone's oil company contracts. When he left, Freddy said he was useless anyway and praised the heavens that he had saved him the trouble of sacking him.

"Still, for all his faults Freddy is never actually spiteful and if one of his ex-teachers asks for his old job back - as happened in my case - he welcomes him with open arms. So if you are planning to desert us don't feel that you have burnt your boats. You can crawl back to him any time with your tail between your legs and he'll wipe the slate clean."

As if to remind Edward that they had not forgotten him, the police suddenly appeared at his door one afternoon while Bob was visiting. This time they were all smiles.

"Hell? Hello mister. How are you? Just another word about the incident if you don't mind."

"Certainly. Any new information?"

"No, nothing. But we'd just like to be sure that Mr. Peter was where he says he was during that afternoon. So far we have only his word for it and your statement that the Egyptian girl confirms he was with her."

"I don't see how you can seriously suspect he might have had something to do with it?"

"No, we don't really. We just want to close the file on our inquiries."

"But I can't see how you can confirm his statement unless you speak to his girlfriend face to face... If you really feel you need proof of his innocence, perhaps we could arrange an informal meeting with her in a public place for a few minutes? Rather than at the police station, I mean."

"Hmm. Good idea. I'm just wondering how we could do it."

"Well, what about... rather than the police station... what about somewhere like the cafe in the Khajal Shopping Centre? You often see girls there together without a male companion, even Arab girls... If she could arrange to be there with a girlfriend - say at four o'clock one afternoon - you and I could turn up a few minutes later as casual acquaintances and just bump into them as if by chance. As she and I know each other from Mottled Oil, she could introduce me as a former colleague and I could introduce you as a friend, and no-one would think it particularly odd if we joined them for a quick cup of coffee."

"That sounds good... All I'll have to do now is think how to phrase the questions so that they sound like normal conversation rather than a grilling, and then coach you to ask them rather than me. Do you think you could manage that? Meanwhile Mr. Peter can explain to her about the plan. Of course, the girlfriend will have to be someone who knows about her and Mr. Peter... Here is my number." He handed Edward a card.

"What the hell was all that?" said Bob after they had left.

"That was the police. It's an old story that won't quite go away. Our company's auditor was found dead in the school a few weeks ago - I think it was probably before you came out here - and it seems his death was not due to natural causes. None of us at Monotone are seriously under suspicion, but the police haven't tied up all the loose ends yet."

"Most intriguing. You must tell me all about it some time. Anyway, the reason I called by was to say that your job application has been officially approved now and all that remains is the Minister's signature on the letter of appointment. I think it's time you told your boss about it so that he can make arrangements to find a new manager and recruit two English teachers instead of three. Otherwise it wouldn't be fair on him."

That evening Edward called Freddy, with much trepidation, to give him the news.

"Believe me Freddy, whatever I may have said to various people, I never really planned to leave Monotone. The college made me an offer and my immediate instinct was to turn them down, but then they started pressing me."

"Sorry. I don't believe you. In any case, you could have said no."

"I know, but they assured me they would make it worth your while and they said they wanted me to join them because I'm an expatriate who knows the country. All their UN staff are new here and still feeling their way."

"I can't see how they can make poaching you worth our while, but still..."

"Anyway, I've always been happy with Monotone and as I say the thought of leaving had never seriously occurred to me. It's just that..."

"Listen, you've said quite enough! Don't bother trying to justify yourself."

"I'm not. I'm just trying to explain."

"Will they be paying you more?"

"A bit more than I'm being paid now, but the main thing is that the holidays are longer and it's a five-day week with fixed working hours."

"I see... It sounds to me as if you are being enticed rather than pressured. Poached in fact, with your full connivance."

"No, that's not true. As far as I'm concerned, these are minor considerations... And whatever happens to me in the future, I'll always be proud to have been part of the Monotone family."

At this point Freddy softened slightly.

"Well, it's your life and I can't stop you. But whatever the temptations I'm sure you'll find the grass is no greener on their side of the fence than it is on ours... We'll have to talk later. All I can say now is that I'm surprised at you and I'll need to get my head round this... Now what about your successor? Do you think any of your Monotone colleagues in Khajal would be able to take over from you or should we recruit someone here in London?"

Edward said he would talk to Roy Sladen and see if he was interested.

A few days later he rang the police station to ask what was happening about the staged meeting with Salma. He had started to have doubts about the plan and he was not surprised to learn that the police felt the same way.

"On consideration, the whole idea makes no sense at all," the officer in charge of the case told him. "If the Egyptian girl confirms Mr. Peter's statement, that wouldn't prove anything. It could just mean that he'd told her to say he had been with her."

"Yes. That had occurred to me too," Edward said. "Though of course I know perfectly well that he couldn't possibly be guilty of anything like murder. He's one of the gentlest people I..."

"That's another point. We really have no reason whatsoever to suspect him. He only came to our notice in the first place because he was absent from the training centre during the crucial time, but there is no evidence that he ever knew the victim Mr. ... Marrows?"

"Maurice."

"Marrows. Yes, Mr. Marrows. Mr. Peter is a teacher and Mr. Marrows was an auditor, so there is really no connection between them."

"Exactly. Our teachers have nothing to do with our company's finances. They just teach and get paid their salaries at the end of the month."

"And on top of all that, the whole plan is too complicated. In my experience complicated plans nearly always go wrong. We can't be sure that all the people involved will turn up punctually at the place they are expected to be. And you and I would have to be reasonably good actors - competent enough to convince the Egyptian girlfriend's girlfriend that our meeting was purely by chance, and also to direct the conversation in a way that would make it appear spontaneous and natural."

So the plan was scrapped and Peter was quietly dropped from the list of suspects. As he had been the only person left on the list by this stage the police were now completely in the dark and had no idea where to turn next.

As far as Edward's replacement was concerned, things proceeded apace. Roy Sladen agreed to take over as manager, Mike Kelly agreed, somewhat reluctantly, to take over from Roy as senior teacher at Mottled Oil and Freddy recruited a new teacher in London to replace Mike. Meanwhile, two promising candidates ("brilliant and ideal for the job", according to Freddy) had been signed up to join Edward on the technical college project.

Edward felt a deep sense of relief at the seamless way the transition was working out and when Bob called round unexpectedly one evening to see him he was pondering contentedly over life after Monotone.

"Bit of a hitch I'm afraid," Bob told him. He looked uneasy.

"??" said Edward's eyebrows.

"Erm, it's about you joining us. There's been a hitch."

"Serious?"

"I'm afraid so. The Minister has decided to reject your application. I tried to get him to relent but he was adamant."

"My God! Why? This puts me in a terrible spot!"

"I'm afraid it's partly my fault... Entirely my fault actually. When I went to see the Minister this morning I casually mentioned that visit you had from the police a couple of weeks ago. I was just making conversation and I thought it was rather an amusing story..."

"I can see where this is heading," Edward said.

"Well, the Minister didn't see it that way. 'He's been in trouble with the police?' he said. 'No, not trouble,' I said. 'Just helping them with their inquiries.' I could have phrased it better, I suppose. 'That means there is a question-mark over him,' the Minister said. 'But he's not suspected of anything himself,' I said. 'Even so, the fact that he is involved in a police inquiry means he's been involved in some kind of trouble and that means he is not the sort of person we want working for us,' he said."

"You know what this means," Edward said. "I've resigned from my job, one of my colleagues is replacing me, a new teacher has been signed up to replace him and now there is nowhere for me to go."

That evening he rang Freddy and explained the situation.

"Well, well, well. I suppose I ought to sympathise, though you really have only yourself to blame," Freddy said. "I told you that you should have stayed with us." He chuckled complacently. "Still, I'm a kind-hearted soul and fortunately I can suggest a solution, though you might not like it much. What do you think of this? Roy takes over from you. (That's already been agreed, of course.) We offer his replacement at Mottled to the technical college as they now have a vacancy (since you're not joining them), and you go back to Mottled as an English teacher. You'll have to take a salary cut but at least you'll have a job."

7.

LIFE BACK AT SQUARE ONE

From Edward's Diary:

12th August 1977

Well, well, well. Here I am back at Mottled Oil. Still working for the same boss in London but this time as an ordinary teacher again (or rather, acting senior teacher; Mike Kelly never really wanted the job in the first place). Of course I've had to accept quite a cut in salary but it's still enough to live on.

Looking back at the lofty heights of my sixteen-month stint in charge of Monotone Khajal's branch, my main feeling today is one of relief that it is all behind me. I am not a natural administrator.

When I first accepted the job I was pretty sure it was going to be a nightmare (which it was on the whole – for me, anyway) and a disaster (which I'm happy to say it wasn't – quite!), but what else could I have done? My "special assignment" with Mottled Oil – a temporary position which their Personnel Manager had offered me as an act of charity when my transfer to Beirut fell through – was about to come to an end, so my only options were branch manager or a one-way ticket back to England.

Now that I am a classroom teacher again, I only have to worry about work during working hours so this leaves me with plenty of time to ponder over my life and review my situation; or rather (more often than not as it turns out), indulge in a daily bout of self-pity and regret for my misspent years since leaving university.

Although I like to think of myself as an altruistic, compassionate sort of fellow, I have to admit that my main concern has always been at least ninety per cent with my own problems and welfare. And these days I'm adding quite a big dose of resentment to my other musings.

A couple of months ago, I was – or thought I was – about to escape from Monotone's clutches and walk into a job at the Gulf Technical College. I wouldn't say it was exactly a plum job, but I would have been in charge of setting up the English courses and I stood a good chance of eventually getting a contract with the ILO –the International Labour Organisation – which would have meant a huge salary and a United Nations passport. (I know a UN passport is of little practical value but it would have been good for the ego.)

However, it all came to nought when the College's project manager made some indiscreet remarks about me to the Minister of Manpower and the Minister – quite unfairly – decided not to employ me after all.

OK. It's true that I haven't got any right to feel hard done by. After all, I have a job. I'm a lot better off than many people I know and I really shouldn't care overmuch about missing out on the prospect of a stratospheric income. If being rich was all that important to me I wouldn't have decided to be a teacher in the first place. Stockbroking or estate agenting perhaps, or some other kind of mind-numbing occupation, would have fitted the bill better. At least my present job is reasonably satisfying and at times I even enjoy it.

But what should I be doing with my life? Can I seriously say that I belong here in Khajal?

The short answer is... Well, actually, there probably isn't a short answer. Not really. I grew up in the south of England, in end-of-empire 1950s and 1960s Britain with its conventional British values and mentality - and I was brought up as a Christian though I'm not sure what I believe now. But that is the world that shaped me.

Khajal, on the other hand, is a different world. But is it really an alien world?

This time I can definitely give a short answer: No it isn't. At least, it doesn't seem alien to me. I've got used to the place and I feel at home here, though I know I'm a foreigner and that if I were a Khajali I would be expected to follow different rules (stricter in some respects, while perhaps allowing more latitude in others).

Of course, much would depend on which Khajali social group I belonged to. Tribal Khajalis are extremely hard-line (to our Western way of thinking) and have certain taboos which I would find unbearable. For one thing, there is rigid gender segregation and if you belong to a tribe you can't do certain jobs, play a musical instrument or do various other things that we in the West regard as normal and natural. I don't think there are any tribal craftsmen – carpenters, silversmiths, plumbers etc. – because the craft professions are despised as inferior occupations for inferior people (perhaps language teaching would also fall into that category?), and there are certainly no tribal waiters, barbers or laundrymen. In fact, even non-tribal Khajalis would be frowned on by their families if they did menial jobs like those. It's just NOT THE DONE THING for a Khajali!

Non-tribal Khajalis generally have more liberal attitudes than their tribal counterparts. Mostly descended from the Sunnis of the coastal region of southern Iran – particularly the Lengeh area – and commonly known as *Huwila* ("Converts"), they describe themselves as "returning Arabs" whose ancestors migrated from Arabia to Iran in the distant past. (This may or may not be true. My tribal Khajali acquaintances say they are actually Iranians, not Arabs.)

If I were an adult Khajali I would be expected to be married and, unless I happened to belong to a very broad-minded family, my nearest and dearest would have the final say (or at least a veto) on my choice of bride. And if I was from a tribal background I probably would not be able to marry a non-tribal girl. (And if I was a tribal girl I certainly wouldn't be able to marry a non-tribal man.)

Even so, despite the rules, restrictions and taboos, I think Khajali families are generally happier than ours in the West. They have a sense of security, whatever their circumstances, and their members support and protect each other through thick and thin even when they step out of line - unless the transgression is too major.

Although I'm not a Muslim, I can't help feeling that Khajalis owe much of their happiness and peace of mind to their Islamic faith. It must be very reassuring to know that life has a purpose and that this world is no more than a transitional stage on the road to eternity. And you only have to look at the serene, contented faces of old Khajalis in their seventies and eighties (and older) to understand that the approach of death holds no terrors for them.

The strong sense of community across the social spectrum regardless of class or tribe, and the self-confidence you find in even the poorest Khajali, also shows that, whatever their social differences, Khajalis share a feeling that they are all brothers and sisters in humanity. And I'm sure this must be because they are united by a common faith.

That there are good people everywhere is undeniable, and I

know that in the West there are still many believing Christians (Although there are fewer nowadays than there used to be some decades ago, the majority of non-believers have inherited Christian ethical values from their parents and grandparents, so I suppose that in a sense one could count them as Christians too), and both Islam and Christianity see charity and compassion as obligatory.

However, Christians tend to be a bit vague about what precisely this means. While Islam defines, in chapter and verse, the way that Muslims are expected to behave in their temporal as well as spiritual lives (including the percentage of their wealth they are required to give to those in need), Christianity just urges us to be good and kind without going into details; or alternatively, it tells us to give away all our possessions to the poor – a suggestion that an average normal person would regard as pretty unrealistic.

As I say, I'm not a Muslim but I can't help feeling that in many ways their religion is superior to ours. I remember a discussion with my Khajali friend Salim (a strong believer, though not always a particularly upright one), when he said (though not in precisely these words; his English is only post-intermediate level, so I have polished it up a bit):

"Of course I respect the Christian religion. After all, Jesus the Messiah – may peace be upon him – was sent by Allah as a messenger to mankind. But from what I hear I get the feeling Christianity is nearly all about going to church or saying an occasional prayer. It's quite big on the spiritual side, but it doesn't tell people how they should live their lives on earth. I'm sure that's the main reason why if you look at history you will find Christians have been guilty of far worse atrocities against their fellow human beings than we Muslims ever have. Even against their fellow Christians. Unlike us, they haven't been instructed in the ethics of war and conflict. And whatever our shortcomings as Arabs today, Muslim societies have traditionally provided much better care and support for those in need than even the modern welfare states in the West. Islam..."

"Nonsense," I said. "You're just making a lot of sweeping statements. And as for atrocities, what about Tamerlane? He was a Muslim, wasn't he?"

"Who?"

"Tamerlane. A ruler from Samarkand... I think it was Samarkand. He massacred millions of people in the lands he conquered and built pyramids out of his victims' skulls."

"Oh, you mean Timur? He was an exception. It's true that he called himself a Muslim but everyone knows he was a Muslim in name only. Anyway he was descended from Genghis Khan so what could you expect? Saladin is a much better example. An upright, honourable Muslim leader who even his Christian enemies liked and respected... Listen... As I was about to say when you interrupted me, Islam tells you how to live your worldly life while preparing yourself for the life to come. Ali bin Abi Talib – the Prophet's cousin and son-in-law – summed it up in one sentence: 'Live for this world as if you will live for ever, and live for the next as if you will die tomorrow'. I don't think I need to explain what he meant."

"Hmm... No, please explain," I said. "I would have thought it should be the other way round."

"No. What he was saying was that you are living in this world now so you should live your life in it to the full and give it one hundred per cent. However, you should never forget that you could die at any time. That means you should always be prepared for death and make sure that the life you live on earth is as upright and blameless as possible. Then when you face Allah on the Day of Judgement you will not be held to account for your sins."

Anyway, to return to more mundane matters ...

Roy, my successor as Khajal branch manager, seems to be getting on OK so far and my impression is that he is comfortable enough in his new post. Still, he always felt he could do a better job than me so I suppose now he is happy that he has a chance to prove it.

It is only about six weeks since he took over and he hasn't had to deal with any real crises yet, though I have to admit (reluctantly) that in many ways he is actually better managerial material than I am. He is quite efficient (more organised and efficient than me anyway), the important customers (like Mottled's Personnel Manager and the head of army training) already think he is amazing and he is less prone to panic than me.

The only thing I fear is that he may not be tough enough to stand up to Freddy. I have warned him that Freddy is constantly pressing the Khajal branch (Monotone's main cash cow) to send him more money than it can afford to and I can say with some confidence that when I was in the driving seat I was usually able to resist his more unreasonable demands.

One of Freddy's favourite ploys is to ask for a large short-term "loan" to be repaid "within weeks", which of course he never pays back. A couple of years ago the manager of our neighbouring branch fell for this and the consequence was within a hair's breadth of catastrophic. The branch went into debt, its cheques started to bounce and Freddy regretfully declined to lift a finger to help ("I'm sorry Chris, but you should really be more prudent about the way you handle your branch's account").

Fortunately, the bank was uncharacteristically understanding when Chris explained the situation to them (uncharacteristically, because Monotone has a bad reputation in the banking community and its accounts are kept on a tight leash) and the branch managed to survive, though it suffered nearly a year of extreme anxiety and damage to its commercial reputation before it was able to consider itself out of danger.

I expect Freddy will give Roy a bit of time to find his feet before he tries anything on with him.

25th August 1977

Roy is giving us all a twenty per cent pay rise from next month. I increased it slightly a while ago when George Weever agreed to put up our fee from Mottled Oil, but my colleagues said it wasn't nearly enough and from then on my relations with them, which had already begun to deteriorate for one reason or another, went from bad to worse.

Consequently, the news that Roy was taking over from me was welcomed by one and all and now I suppose he feels he's got to live up to their expectations. They felt he was on their side, while I had come to be seen as Freddy's lackey. Most unfair. My only concern was to ensure that the branch remained solvent.

I was afraid Roy might do something like this. Although I had told him repeatedly that the wide gap between Monotone's fees from its customers and its staff salaries, rents and air fares should not be seen as clear profit, and despite my warning that appearances could be deceptive and "contingencies" were often surprisingly expensive, he insisted that I was being absurdly over-cautious.

"I felt the same way as you at first but I can assure you that you'll change your mind before very long when you've seen how things work out in practice," I told him. Anyway, he is in charge now and I wouldn't like him to feel I'm constantly looking over his shoulder or undermining his authority, so from now on I'm going to keep my views to myself. I'm not afraid he'll sack me or anything, but I like and respect him, he already knows what I think and the last thing I want is to poison my relations with him and my colleagues, whom I still regard as friends despite the recent tensions between us.

One interesting aspect of all this is how Freddy will react to the big pay rise. He's never been a great fan of "pampering the staff", as he calls it, and of course Roy will have to tell him what he is doing. It's not something you can keep secret from your boss.

10ᵗʰ September 1977

Freddy's reaction was quite interesting. Somewhat unexpected, but on second thoughts I think very much in character really as I can see where it is heading. According to Roy, he said:

"Well of course it's your business to run your branch in the way you see fit. If you really have to pay them that much more, no doubt you have good reasons and as the man on the spot I'm sure you know best... I've always felt you have better sense in these matters than Edward did. He was almost pathologically afraid of loosening the purse strings... and you and I have a much healthier attitude. Money is to be used – appropriately, of course – and not stashed away in the bank where it's doing no good to anyone."

"So you see, Edward, I know what I'm doing and Freddy approves," Roy told me cheerfully.

"OK. Fine. You're the boss," I said.

"You're looking rather sceptical. What do you really think?"

"All right... Well, don't take this as sour grapes or anything, but – to be frank - you seem to think Freddy's support is a vindication of your extravagance (you may not call it that, but that's how I see it). I'm not saying a twenty per cent pay rise is going to bankrupt us but you're leaving very little room for dealing with nasty surprises. And believe me, they do happen. Things may be OK as long as we don't have another disaster like the Barrett saga... or lose a contract due to some cock-up on our part. But there's no guarantee something like that won't happen."

"Well, we've just got to keep our eye on the ball then and make sure it doesn't."

"...And another reason Freddy seems to be encouraging you to loosen the purse strings, as he puts it, is that he's almost certainly softening you up for a big touch from London. And that's something we definitely can't afford now."

"What do you mean?"

"He hasn't put the squeeze on you yet, but it won't be long before he starts telling you to send him more money on top of our regular monthly transfers. Money we can ill afford at the best of times. All that ever matters to him is short-term gain. The fact that he might sink us completely over the mid to longer term... I wouldn't say it never occurs to him, but he refuses to think about it when there is an immediate prospect of a few thousand extra pounds in his pocket. And if you refuse to cough up when he approaches you he will tell you that of course you can manage it if you are able to give your staff a twenty per cent pay rise."

It's lucky Roy and I are friends. He didn't take offence and I could see that he accepted my comments as well intentioned, if perhaps unduly pessimistic.

Or possibly not unduly pessimistic. I thought he looked pensive.

12th October 1977

Roy came to see me yesterday evening after work in a bit of a state. He had had a call from London that afternoon with a request for money without delay:

"Sorry Roy. I wouldn't normally do this", Freddy told him (He would, of course. He does it all the time). "But you're the man to help us out. We've got an unforeseen emergency on our hands here in London at the moment and we need a loan urgently... Otherwise... I won't go into detail, but the bailiffs will be round within the next day or two and we'll lose all our furniture and office equipment. I would ask our other branches to chip in too, but they've got troubles of their own and Khajal is the only one with a bit of spare cash."

"Oh Freddy, I'm really sorry. Of course we'll do anything we can to help."

"As I say, it would only be a loan... for a month or six weeks. Two months absolute max. Don't worry. You'll get it back. Trust me."

"I thought... well, furniture and office equipment... a few hundred pounds should cover that," Roy told me. "So I said to him: 'How much do you need? Would five hundred pounds do it?' His reply was a mirthless laugh.

"That wouldn't even start to cover it, I'm afraid. You see, we're behind with the rent as well so we're facing the possibility of eviction in the near future. I was thinking of something in the region of three thousand."

That really shook me.

"Pounds?" I said. "Or riyals?"

"Pounds of course. But don't worry. You'll get it back. As I say, it's only a short-term loan. All you'll have to do is hang on for a bit till your next payments come in from Mottled and the army. In your situation you shouldn't even need to ask the bank for an overdraft."

I must say I've never seen Roy look so worried.

"Did you ever have to get an overdraft?" he asked me.

"No. The bank – not just this branch but the other branches too – has been dealing with Freddy for years and it knows exactly what he's like, so they've erected red flags around the Monotone accounts... luckily we've always been comfortably in credit here in Khajal. Apart from one very short period of about two or three days just before I took over when Mottled's payment arrived late after they switched to a new accounting system."

I've suggested to Roy that he should send Freddy what he can up to a maximum of about eight hundred pounds and explain that the bank is being difficult about overdrafts. A flat refusal is out. Even I had to send Freddy occasional sums on top of our regular payments and I pride myself that I was quite tough with him. Hence his snide remark about my fear of loosening the purse strings.

17th October 1977

In the end, after a series of fraught telephone calls with Head Office, Roy sent Freddy just over two thousand pounds. It probably won't kill us but it puts us in a dicey situation and we may have to delay next month's regular remittance, which Freddy won't like one bit.

Roy and I are the only people here in Khajal who know what is going on. There's no need to frighten the rest of the staff because it is the manager's job to worry about such things, not theirs. That's the main reason why a manager is on a higher salary. On the other hand, Roy is right to share his troubles with me because, as the ex-manager, I understand the situation and may be able to offer some useful advice (if he wants it, of course - and provided that things don't deteriorate beyond repair).

20th October 1977

This morning I was talking to Saud – one of our mature students on temporary release from the Finance Department – about the tragedy we had earlier this year. Maurice, our company auditor who had just arrived here on a two-day visit, died in mysterious circumstances in the school and the pathologist's report indicated that foul play was involved. For a time one or two of us at Monotone were in the frame, though in the absence of any evidence or motive the case was dropped. Or rather, not exactly dropped but left open and classed as an unsolved suspected homicide.

I mentioned to Saud that at the early stage of the investigation even I had been asked to account for my movements and he said he would ask a friend of his, who is a senior police officer, if there had been any further developments recently.

21st October 1977

A rather odd new twist to the tale. Saud rang his friend yesterday and learnt that the whole thing was a mistake due to a mix-up at the hospital. Or by the police (The police say the hospital was to blame). Whoever's fault it was, the paperwork somehow got swapped around so that Maurice's supposed post-mortem report was in fact for the victim of a motor-cycle accident (also a Western expatriate), while his actual report showed no evidence of foul play and recorded the cause of death as a heart attack. His skull hadn't been fractured and the external bleeding probably occurred because the skin at the back of his head was broken when his head hit an uneven floor tile.

So we at Monotone are completely in the clear now.

28th October 1977

Far be it from me to criticise other people's drinking habits - I like a drink myself - but my housemate Mike Kelly has been overdoing it a bit recently (When Roy took over from me as manager he and I swapped accommodation as well as jobs, so now he is living above the school and I've moved into the villa with Mike).

Mike was fine until a few weeks ago when he discovered Glen Reuben - a dubious pale yellow liquor that calls itself whisky, though it hails from Stepney, not Scotland, and gives off a faint odour of paraffin, not single malt. Its only positive feature is its price. It is so cheap that Mike has been able to increase the volume of his monthly alcohol allowance by nearly half, but I think it may be seriously damaging his brain.

Last Thursday I was woken up by an almighty crash at one o'clock in the morning and a voice exclaiming "Cheeses!"; at least, that's what I thought it was saying, possibly because I had just been dreaming about a family dinner party. I turned on my bedside light and saw Mike rising slowly from the floor, surrounded by the wreckage of my upturned occasional table, a chair on its side, four shattered tea glasses, my coffee mug and my large enamel teapot.

"What the hell's going on?" I asked sleepily. "And why did you say 'Cheeses'?"

"What do you mean 'Cheeses'? I was saying 'Jesus!' because I'd fallen over your table. Why did you leave it there? Bloody stupid place to put it."

"What are you doing in my room anyway? Do you know what time it is?"

"There's a huge rat sitting on my bed. As big as a tomcat. Come and get rid of it for me... Please. You know I can't stand rats."

Mike is paranoid about rats and Khajal has a serious rat problem, but although they are frequent visitors to the garden, I've never actually seen one inside the house.

I got out of bed and accompanied Mike to his room, which yielded no sign of a rat whatsoever – not on the bed, under the bed or anywhere else.

"Are you sure you didn't imagine it?" I said.

"Of course I didn't. How could anyone imagine a rat?"

We checked the rest of the house. When we had established that it too was totally ratless, we retired to our beds.

Mike looked as fresh as a daisy before we set off for work the next morning and I asked him how he was feeling.

"Fine," he said. "Why shouldn't I be?"

"Well, I was thinking about that business with the rat."

"What rat?"

"The one you found on your bed."

"A rat on my bed? What are you talking about?"

"When you came into my room in the middle of last night and woke me up and said there was a rat on your bed."

"I did no such thing! I never saw a rat. I would have remembered if I had. You must have dreamt it."

"Come on now. Are you trying to tell me you've forgotten? You smashed my tea glasses when you tripped over my table. If you don't believe me, go and look in the bin in the kitchen."

Even the little collection of shards failed to convince him.

"Nothing to do with me," he said. "You must have done it yourself."

*   *   *   *

The night before last I was woken up again in the small hours; this time Mike was in my room wrestling with the door of my wardrobe, which I always keep locked.

"What...?" I inquired. "These nocturnal visits are becoming rather a habit with you. What is it this time?"

"Why is this bathroom door stuck? I can't get it open and I'm bursting for a slash."

I got out of bed and guided him to the bathroom, then led him back to his bed.

As on the previous occasion, when I mentioned the subject over coffee the next morning he insisted it had never happened and that I must have dreamt it.

25th November 1977

Although he won't admit it in so many words, Roy is beginning to regret the twenty per cent pay rise, but he realises it is too late to do anything about it. Just imagine what would happen if he called a staff meeting and announced he was cancelling it because it had all been a mistake!

Fingers crossed, we should be OK if nothing truly disastrous happens and he manages to keep Freddy off his back. In most other respects I think he is doing rather a good job and his colleagues are certainly happy with him.

15ᵗʰ December 1977

Mike has bought another second-hand car. He owned one a while back but had to sell it when it was discovered his driving licence was phoney (he was only partly to blame for this) and he was stung with a very hefty fine. He was lucky he wasn't sent to prison. The authorities here take a dim view of forged documents, particularly when they purport to come from official Khajali government departments.

Since then he has managed to get a *bona fide* licence through the proper channels.

16ᵗʰ December 1977

Peter used to pick us up from our homes and take us to work, but the arrangement was quietly dropped in the middle of last year when he went back to England for his summer holiday and it was never renewed. After I moved in with Mike, we had a standing arrangement with a local taxi driver, but it wasn't a hundred per cent satisfactory because our driver had a rather relaxed attitude to punctuality and sometimes he didn't turn up at all if he had something better or more important to attend to.

However, now that Mike has a car, we no longer have any worries about getting to work on time. I have offered to pay him the equivalent of the cost of the taxi, but he said he would be happy to take me for free as we both work at the same place. I told him that was very generous, much appreciated etc., but that I couldn't agree to it because it wouldn't be fair on him, so we have now decided that I will pay my share of the petrol and make an occasional contribution to any other running costs.

Although I find it handy having a housemate with a car, Glen Reuben seems to be taking over Mike's life these days and I'm worried that he might decide to go out one evening when he has had a few too many and get stopped by the police. I've heard of several Westerners being deported for drunken driving recently.

3rd January 1978

Freddy has been pressing Roy for another substantial "loan" and when Roy tried to put his foot down he got quite nasty. Possibly it was a bit tactless of Roy to suggest that the first "loan" should be paid off first before any further "*ex gratia* transfers" were forthcoming (his words, not mine).

"May I remind you that I am the proprietor of this establishment, not you, and the sole reason why you are the Khajal branch manager is because I have decided you should be? If you insist on treating it as your own private company, I shall have no option but to replace you," Freddy told him. "And apart from anything else, you clearly haven't got a clue about how to handle the account. Khajal ought to be comfortably in profit and the fact that it is not is entirely due to your mismanagement... Edward was far more competent than you are..."

Poor Roy! Now he has caved in again and sent Freddy another fifteen hundred pounds, although he knows it is going to put us in a very difficult situation.

In fact, I'm not quite sure there will be enough in the bank to cover this month's salaries.

31st January 1978

We have managed to pay the salaries but this has left us a few hundred riyals short for the rents, which are due in a week's time. We just may take enough in school fees before then, but there is no certainty and I am going to suggest to Roy that he has a word with the bank manager. This branch has never been overdrawn before (well, almost never) and they might agree to a short-term overdraft.

1st February 1978

Success! (For the moment anyway.) We have had to go slightly into the red but with the bank's consent we now have a four thousand riyal overdraft facility till 3rd March.

We should manage to survive if Roy can fend off Freddy's threats and blandishments from now on. ("Survive". I never thought I would find myself using that word in connection with Monotone Khajal. This is the first time we have ever been in such a situation.)

18th February 1978

A black day. Yesterday evening Mike had Yahya, a Khajali friend from out of town, round for drinks and, as he (Yahya) was a little the worse for wear after he had had a few for the road, Mike insisted on giving him a lift home. I strongly suggested that we should get him a taxi, but to no avail.

"What are friends for?" Mike said. "Yahya's my mate and I'm not going to leave him at the mercy of some stranger in his condition."

When I went to bed at about ten o'clock Mike had still not returned, but I was not surprised or concerned because Yahya's village is over ten miles away and he had only been gone for about an hour.

However, I was more than a little worried when I got up this morning and found that I was still alone in the house. I rang Roy before setting off in search of a taxi to work and told him.

"What sort of state was Mike in when he left?" Roy asked me.

"A bit boisterous perhaps. I wouldn't say he was absolutely stone cold sober, but he seemed more or less all right. I'd say he was definitely *compos mentis*."

Roy said he would check with the hospital and the police and let me know as soon as he heard anything.

At the Mottled Oil Training Centre I would normally have been free for the first lesson, but Mike was supposed to be teaching so I had to cover for him. Naturally, the trainees were curious about why there had been a change of teacher and I tried – not very successfully, I fear – to conceal the fact that I was as mystified as they were about where Mike had got to.

At about 9 o'clock Roy appeared, looking grim.

"Well, I've managed to locate him," he said.

"Is he OK?"

"He's alive and conscious but in hospital and very badly injured. I'm told he has some organ damage – I don't know how serious - and he is completely blind in one eye and half blind in the other. At the moment they are trying to find out if there is any chance of restoring his sight, but it seems the best they can hope for is that it doesn't get any worse than it is already... and his leg has been broken in two places, but that's almost a minor detail."

This is an unmitigated disaster. If I had the words to express it more strongly than that I would use them. Mike is barely in his early thirties but with life-changing injuries like these I fear he may never be able to work again. I can't imagine what my feelings would be if I found myself in his position.

And on top of all this, it could well mean curtains for Monotone Khajal.

"What about Yahya, his passenger?" I asked.

"He's in hospital too, but apart from slight concussion and a few cuts and bruises his only real injury seems to be a broken nose.

They are keeping him in for checks, but he'll probably be given the all-clear later today."

"Did you discover what happened?"

"According to the police, Mike says he thinks a large animal suddenly appeared in front of him out of nowhere. He swerved to avoid it but hit a boulder beyond the hard shoulder and overturned. A few minutes later, according to Yahya, they were spotted by a couple of passing patrolmen who saw the car upside down by the roadside and called the traffic police and emergency services... Another thing, of course, is that Mike's blood test showed he had drunk quite a lot of alcohol, which I imagine will not look good on any insurance claim."

As well as being a personal calamity for Mike (though "calamity" can't begin to describe the gravity of his situation), the implications for Monotone's future are truly frightening. Our pay increase and Roy's recent "loans" to Freddy in London have left us no room at all for manoeuvre and now we have been landed with enormous costs that we have no chance of meeting. Even if we were comfortably in the black it would still need a rescue operation. Forget the loss of fees from Mottled until we can find a replacement. Far more serious is the cost of repatriating Mike, which will be enormous as he will have to travel with a trained nurse/companion and proper medical support equipment, and this will probably mean reserving a whole section of the plane. All at Monotone's expense, of course.

I know that he has no medical insurance himself and Monotone has never bothered with any kind of cover for its staff. During his last visit here I remember Freddy boasting about how he was able to operate so much more cheaply than his competitors because he didn't go in for what he called "fringe expenditures" ("Believe me, the odds against something truly major happening are so remote that we would just be putting money into the insurance companies' pockets. Anything less than that we can cover ourselves").

20th February 1978

Roy is in despair. George Weever is sympathetic and he says he will do whatever he can to help within reason, but that he can't pretend we still have a full quota of Monotone teachers at Mottled Oil when we haven't; the hard-headed men at Mottled's head office would never buy it. Still, I get the feeling that he is genuinely trying to think of some constructive suggestions.

Freddy is in a state of shock and says he will get back to us, though Roy suspects his top priority at present is to find a way of dumping us with minimum damage to himself and the rest of his business. But at least he is not blaming Roy's management for the disaster. Our colleagues, on the other hand, are furious with Roy. They hold him totally responsible for our plight and, with the benefit of hindsight, they are now saying they already had doubts about his competence when he first decided to give them such a big pay rise.

In the meantime, we are doing our best to carry on as normal, though our classroom performance has been noticeably below par over the past couple of days. The trainees have been very understanding and are most upset about what has happened. Mike was probably the most popular teacher on our team.

24th February 1978

Pay day is approaching and this month we should all receive our salaries. The problem is what is going to happen next. One option being considered is for Mottled and the army to take us on under six-month direct contracts. That would give us some respite personally but it wouldn't save Monotone Khajal. However, Freddy says he is "working on it".

Mike is now able to receive visitors throughout the day, but the ward sister only lets us stay for a few minutes at a time as he is still very weak. He gets regular visits and messages from the trainees, which he says means a lot to him. It is hard to tell what he really feels, but at the moment he just seems relieved that he is still alive and he is not too pessimistic about his future.

"I don't think I'll be dependent on others for the rest of my life," he told me when I went to see him today. "I can see well enough to function, though my field of vision is very limited and of course I can't judge distances because for all intents and purposes I've only got one eye. I know the other eye looks all right but it might as well be glass for all the use it is."

26th February 1978

Things are moving fast. Freddy has been putting the word around and Global Schools – a large, well-funded, London-based language-teaching company with branches throughout Europe and in several Middle Eastern countries – has expressed an interest in buying Monotone Khajal from him. Despite our present dire situation, we are still potentially a profitable operation and the rumour is that Freddy is going to offer us to them at a knock-down price.

1st March 1978

The latest we have heard is that Global Schools have proposed they should take over the Khajal branch along with its staff, its assets (which, such as they are, consist basically of our contracts and our rather dodgy reputation) and its present and short-term future liabilities, including the astronomical cost of repatriating Mike. Freddy would not receive any cash from them, but they are prepared to pay off Monotone's London debts too, leaving him with a clean sheet to start again - and no doubt build up a new lot of financial crises for himself and Monotone in the not-too-distant future, as he will have no longer have the Khajal branch to bail him out. He is considering the offer and we believe he is likely to accept.

Global run a much tighter and more professional ship than Monotone. We think that, assuming Freddy agrees, this will generally be to our advantage, though we are wondering if our salaries and working conditions are likely to be affected.

4th March 1978

Freddy has accepted Global's offer. We will probably not notice any difference in the immediate future. Our jobs are secure, Mottled, the army and our other customers are happy and Roy will remain in place for the time being until Global can send out their own man to replace him. After that he will probably join Freddy and the team in London until they decide what to do with him.

8.

MONOTONE GOES GLOBAL

I t was the beginning of April. Monotone Khajal was now Global Schools (Khajal) and Mike Kelly had been flown back to England at great expense. Global's Middle East area director – a tubby, grey-haired man in a beige suit who smelled slightly of Paco Rabanne aftershave – had just arrived on a two-day visit to meet the customers and teaching staff ("Hello there, friends and new colleagues. My name's Tom Pryke... It's a real delight to be here in Cadgel. Wonderful country, super people. Can't tell you how much I've been looking forward to this visit") and assure the latter ("apart from friend Roy here") that their jobs were safe.

"Nick Hoskins, your new manager, will be here within the next couple of weeks and of course you will all help him to settle in, won't you? He's a super chap. Background in business management, not teaching, but if there's one thing he knows about, it's dealing with people... and at the end of the day, that's what really matters. That's the name of the game, isn't it?" Tom told them in plummy tones. "He'll leave you to get on with your thing - provided that the customers are happy of course, ha-ha - and you can leave the admin side in his capable hands."

"Will he be running the school in the afternoons and evenings? You know, organising the classes and assessment tests and that sort of thing?" Steve Kettle inquired. "As you know, it needs someone who can produce a timetable and at least tell the difference between elementary, intermediate and advanced."

"It'll be no good asking any of us to do it. Edward, Steve and I don't mind taking on an hour or two of after-hours teaching at the school but that is as far as we are prepared to go," Peter Frazer said. "We'll have already done a full day's work by then."

"Nick's a capable fellow. He can turn his hand to anything. After all, adaptability is the name of the game, isn't it?" said Tom. "And I'm sure your part-time teacher – Jean, is it? – won't mind giving him a hand occasionally if necessary."

The staff looked sceptical.

"Don't you worry about Nick" Tom insisted emphatically, his posh accent slipping briefly into his native Suffolkese as he realised he had a bit of sales resistance to overcome. "As Oi say, there are foo things he can't turn his hand to. He's a proactive fellow. The sort of guy who can think outside the box."

*   *   *   *

"Well, what do you think?" said Steve. He, Peter and Edward were sitting in the "Cornish Café" – a dusty open-air teashop on Khajal City's Corniche. Tom Pryke had retired to his hotel for the evening and was due to fly back to London the following morning. As usual, Dick, the other member of the Mottled Training Centre team, was otherwise engaged. He got on well with his colleagues but moved in different social circles outside work.

"I always thought Monotone were the ultimate shysters, but now I'm not so sure. I suspect they're probably no worse than most of their rivals," Peter said. "Tom's clearly a phoney – a slimy third-rater. 'At the end of the day, adaptability's the name of the game when you think outside the box proactively!' That kind of off-the-peg corporate crap-speak makes me want to throw up. And if he is a typical Global executive, then it seems pretty obvious to me that these people are only interested in their balance-sheets... Or... bean counting is probably what they would call it in their jargon. That sort don't give a damn about teaching. You would have thought he might have asked us a few questions about what we actually do, wouldn't you? About our courses and students? But no. When he came to Mottled this morning his only port of call was George Weever's office. He didn't even visit us at the Training Centre. All he and his kind are interested in is money, money, money... And..."

"So you didn't like him very much... Nor did I for that matter," Edward interjected, "though I'd say he's more a slick salesman than a balance-sheet type. But to give them their due, Global do run a successful operation. Whatever their real motives might be, they have a decent reputation. Their school in Bournemouth is supposed to be one of the best in the country and their founder and chairman – what's his name, Robert Strawmaker? - has an impressive record himself as a course writer and English teacher. In fact, I think he still teaches a bit."

"...And I thought that sly, conniving smile he gave us was particularly offensive. You know, when he made that pointed dig at poor old Roy and said that 'apart from Roy's' our jobs were safe," Peter continued.

"What? ... Are you still banging on about Tom Pryke? ... Just a minute though... A few weeks ago you said Roy was a useless waste of space and you would never forgive him for the mess he had left us in" Edward said.

"That was then. I was very angry at the time. Well, we all were, weren't we, but I'm sure we've forgiven him now– I certainly have

- and he was a great director of studies... No offence, Edward. You've done a good job too, but you know what I mean... I can't see why he shouldn't come back to his old position at Mottled. We've been a teacher short since Mike's accident and it seems ridiculous to bring someone new out from London when we've already got a perfectly good candidate here in Khajal."

The others agreed.

"Of course, it will depend on what Roy himself wants, but I suggest we ask Freddy to recommend him to Global for the Mottled vacancy," Peter said.

So they suggested it to Freddy and Freddy recommended Roy to Global.

"Thanks for touching base, Freddy, but we've already decided we're going to put our own man in place on that contract," Tom told him. "No reflection on Monotone but out there in Cadgel Mottled Oil are our main customers – our big beasts, so to speak - and we think Global ought to raise its profile with them and get its feet under their table pronto. At this moment in time we've got a good candidate lined up for the job. Sorry about Roy and all that, but no can do, Oi'm afraid."

As promised, the new branch manager arrived with his wife a fortnight after Tom's visit and Roy and Edward met them at the airport. A smartly-dressed, athletic-looking youngish man with short blond hair and eyes rather close together, they recognised him instantly from the photograph Global had sent them a few days earlier.

"Nick Hoskins, originally from Australia. Now UK resident and citizen of the world, for my sins. And this is Christine, my better half... Great to be here in Cadgel at last," he gushed with just a trace of an Australian accent. "I've been so much looking forward to meeting you all... And by the way, I come bearing good news. Julian Beardsley, your new senior teacher, will be joining you on the Mottled team next week. They tell me he's champing at the bit and can't wait to get started."

"I can't quite put my finger on it. He's got something of Freddy about him... his appearance mainly... but the person he really reminds me of is Tom. His aura of smugness and bumptious manner perhaps? An addiction to clichés? I don't know. Anyway, I think I'm starting to recognize the Global managerial type," Edward said to himself.

"We've put you and Christine in a hotel for tonight," Roy said as they set off for the town. "I'll be getting out of the manager's flat tomorrow morning, so you can move in there any time. I don't think you'll find it too cramped. Not in the short term anyway. Later you might decide you want somewhere with a bit more room."

"And what about you? Where will you go?" Christine asked.

"I'm moving in with Edward in the villa till the new man arrives. After that I'll go back to London."

"I think we'll have an informal staff meeting tomorrow evening," Nick said. "There are loads of things we need to talk about. But don't worry. There are no really big changes in the pipeline for the immediate future – that's to say, not for today or tomorrow - though as you know we at Global have our own vision of how we want things to be and it's not always quite the same as Monotone's."

"I wonder what changes he has in mind," Roy said after they had dropped Nick and Christine off at the Khajal Palace Hotel. "I'm relieved in a way that I won't be here to see them, though I imagine working more or less in Freddy's pocket isn't exactly going to be a barrel of laughs either. Although he's promised me a job at head office he hasn't said anything about what it will involve or how much he is going to pay me. Or indeed if he is going to pay me anything at all."

*　　*　　*　　*

The staff meeting took place at the school after the last lesson. Apart from Roy, who was no longer involved in the branch's business, all the old Monotone staff were there including Jean (the part-timer) and the army teacher Richard Waite, who lived in army accommodation and generally had little contact with his other colleagues.

"I'd like to start the ball rolling by saying it's great to meet you all. You're doing a fabulous job here and your efforts are much appreciated by the big boys in London ... and the big girls too, of course." Nick gave a perfunctory chuckle. "We've got one or two ladies on our board of directors." He smiled and nodded in Jean's direction. Jean shuffled awkwardly.

"Now I think it's rather too late in the evening to have an extended discussion, especially as most of you start work so early in the morning, but there are three things we ought to look at. The first one – I think we can call it an ASAP case – is salaries."

This time all his audience shuffled uncomfortably as it was clear Nick was not about to announce another pay rise.

"It was pretty rash of my predecessor to give you that twenty per cent rise out of the blue last year. In fact, it was a case not so much of... how should I put it..." ("cliché alert" said Edward to himself) "'too little too late'" ("there you are," said Edward to himself) "as 'too much too soon'. Of course we would all like to be coining it. You can't be blamed for that. But a pay rise can only be justified if the income is high enough to cover it and in this case – as you've learnt to your cost – it wasn't.

"Don't worry, I'm not going to cut your salaries this minute or ask you to refund anything you have already received, but there has got to be a review within the next month. At the moment Global is more or less subsidising you and that doesn't make any business sense. And apart from that, you are also being paid more than anyone else in the region for doing the same job, which isn't right."

"Are you saying you're going to cancel our twenty per cent pay rise?" said Peter belligerently. "That would be illegal."

"I think you'll find you are all in legal limbo at the moment." Nick beamed at them, but in a caring sort of way. "One of our top priorities is to get you on contracts with Global which will set out your new terms of employment. Of course, if you don't like them, you can always leave and we'll give you your air tickets back to the UK and the regulation redundancy pay as per the Cadgerly Labour Law."

"Have you thought of asking Mottled to put up their fees?" said Steve.

"We'll be doing that in due course, but I think it is less than a year since they last put them up.

"...Anyway... There's probably not much more we can discuss on that subject at the moment, so we'll get some draft contracts out to you and wait for your feedback.

"Another important thing we should also touch on this evening... Something I've been looking at from afar ever since I learnt I was coming out here... The school. At Global we regard the school as being at the heart of any operation, but here you've always focused on the outside contracts and the school has been very much the poor relation. Almost an afterthought. Apologies if I'm wrong but that's the clear impression I've got about the Cadgel branch. I want to change all that. I don't mean we're going to drop the contracts. Certainly not. Far from it. We'd like to expand them too, but we want the school to be a proper going concern, not just a place that opens for three or four hours a day for English classes – and only English classes. There's so much more that could be done here... We could run morning shorthand and typing courses. Several of our other branches do that. And with so many expatriates out here there must also be a demand for Arabic lessons.

"In the near future I plan to bring out a full-time principal, director or whatever you like to call him (or her but probably him). We'll start by expanding the English classes. I can't believe we're making the most of our opportunities in that regard at the moment. Then once that side of the operation has really started to take off, we will look at our other options and probably recruit a lady from the UK to set up a secretarial programme. In the meantime, I'd like you all to keep your ears to the ground and an eye out for a local who might be interested in teaching Arabic to foreigners. If we can find a decent candidate we'll train him up and then - ha ha - let him loose in the classroom. I'm sure we will have no difficulty pulling in the students."

He paused and looked round at the assembled company.

"Interesting idea. Good luck with it," said Dick.

"Did you say there were three things you wanted to discuss?" Edward asked.

"Yes. The last item was the course material you are using with our contract customers. I just wanted to say that when Julian comes out – for those of you who don't know this already, Julian Beardsley is going to be our new senior teacher at Mottled Oil – he will take a close look at whatever you are teaching with at the moment and decide if any changes are necessary. We at Global normally use our own material because we like to think it is the best.

"I think that's about everything for now. Thank you. And remember my door is always open if you have anything you'd like to discuss with me."

And so ended Global Schools (Khajal)'s first staff meeting.

*   *   *   *

"I thought he was going to say 'class dismissed'", Peter said.

It was half past nine and Edward, Peter and Steve had retired to their usual haunt – the "Cornish Café"- where they were sitting outside in the cool evening air eating chilli omelette wraps and drinking milkless tea – known in Khajal as *chai Sulaimani*.

"Whether you like him or not, he's certainly done his homework and thought things through," Steve said. "I thought that was quite an impressive performance considering that he's only been in this country for twenty-four hours."

"'Hitting the ground running' is probably how he would describe it," said Peter sourly. "Any ideas about how we can fight this pay cut?"

"Not really. I think he's got us over a barrel... God! I hope I'm not starting to sound like him. Perhaps clichéitis is catching," Steve said. "What do you think, Edward?"

"About what? Clichés or salaries? I shouldn't worry about clichés; we all use them all the time. As far as our salaries are concerned I'm quite happy to go along with him, but then I always thought the twenty per cent pay rise was too high. And I assume he isn't planning to pay us less than we were getting before the increase. That would be very stupid and he doesn't strike me as being a stupid person."

* * * *

The following week Nick announced: "Julian's booked to fly out on Sunday. He'll be able to move into the villa straight away as Roy left last Wednesday, so there won't be any need to put him into a hotel... I've never met him myself, so it'll be a first for all of us, though I hear he's very much one of the lads and a keen rugby player like me. A man after my own heart, you might say."

The Khajal Airport welcoming committee consisted of Nick, who was all psyched up to extend an ebullient welcome to a fellow sports enthusiast, Edward, in his capacity as the acting senior teacher on the Mottled Oil contract, and Nick's wife Christine who had come along for the ride. As none of them knew what the new man looked like, Christine had prepared an arty "Welcome to Khajal" placard with his name – MR. JULIAN BEARDSLEY – on it in bold blue letters for them to display at the arrivals gate.

Julian was a pale, willowy young man in his late twenties with long fair hair and a small baldish patch on the crown of his head. He was rather cowed by his reception, particularly Nick's attempt to turn it into a red carpet occasion.

"Hail the conquering hero comes!" Nick proclaimed heartily with a guffaw and a facetious bow before charging forward and seizing Julian's hand in a manly grip. "The boy we've all been waiting for who's going to set the Mottled team alight. The eyes of the world are upon you." Julian flinched slightly and Christine and Edward looked embarrassed.

"Only one small suitcase? You certainly believe in travelling light," Nick said more soberly after an awkward silence.

"Just a few clothes and books," Julian said nervously.

"Is this your first time in the Arab world?" Edward asked as they set off for the villa in Nick's hire car.

"I've never been to the Middle East before but I taught for a few months in Marrakech, which was great. Most of the time I've been in Europe – Greece mainly."

*   *   *   *

"I like him. He seems nice and I think he will fit in well," Edward reported. He and Steve were discussing the day's events in the "Sharaton Coffe House" – another seafront establishment slightly less dingy than the "Cornish Café" that they patronised from time to time when they felt like a change of scene. Meanwhile, Julian was being treated to dinner by Nick and Christine at one of Khajal

City's more salubrious restaurants.

"Though I don't know where Nick got the idea he was a rugby player," Edward added. "I can't imagine anyone less sporty."

"Crossed wires presumably," Steve said. "Perhaps London told Nick about a sporty new teacher they were sending out to one of their other branches and he got the wrong end of the stick and thought they were talking about Julian. Or maybe there are two Julians and the other one really is a *bona fide* rugger bugger."

The next morning, Nick took Julian out to Mottled Oil and introduced him to George Weever. Weever was not expecting a rugby player so he had no preconceived notions about how to react to him and the meeting was easy and cordial. Julian talked intelligently about his previous work experience and realised early on in their conversation that there would be no point in bending Weever's ear with details about the technicalities of language teaching, and Weever assured him that Mottled was a splendid company to work for, "even for those who happen to be on a subcontract arrangement like you chaps". Then Nick took him to the training centre to meet his colleagues and the trainees. Again the general all-round impression was favourable.

Julian spent the rest of the day looking over the course material and decided that – for the time being anyway – it would be pointless to change the classroom books as the teachers were comfortable with them and, from what he had seen so far, what was being taught seemed appropriate.

"The only thing I would suggest for the immediate future is that we replace the present language lab exercises with our Global course. I'm familiar with the stuff you are using at the moment and I know it's OK, but it is a bit out of date and one or two of the dialogues are plain silly."

"Several of them are very silly, I agree," said Edward. "Particularly the one which introduces the expression 'I beg your pardon'."

"Yes. I think I remember that one. You mean when John says to Mary 'Where's my sandwich?' and Mary replies 'It's on the table'. Then John says 'I beg your pardon. What's on the table?'?"

"Yes. That's the one. Roy did a good piss-take version of it last year: 'How are you today?' 'I'm very well.' 'I beg your pardon. Who's very well?' He was thinking of producing a series of drills along those lines and sending them to the publisher."

Julian laughed.

*　　*　　*　　*

"What was life in Marrakech like?" Edward asked him when they were back at the villa. "A bit different from here, I imagine."

"Different from here? I can't really say yet as this time yesterday I was still in the air half way between London and Khajal. Though I think the climate is probably better in Marrakech than here; it was pleasant most of the time I was there. And the food was good, we had plenty of local friends and we used to get some good *kif*."

"*Kif*? What's *kif*?"

"Weed... marijuana. It was illegal but you wouldn't think so. So many people used it, often quite openly. They've got excellent hash there too. What's the scene like in Khajal?"

"In Khajal it's not just illegal, but very illegal. I've heard of people getting arrested for it and being sent down for years but I don't know anyone personally who uses it. If you're thinking of smoking it here, my advice would be forget it."

Julian was silent.

"Is Marrakech generally a nice place to live?" Edward inquired. "I've never been to Morocco but in pictures it looks more exotic and Arabian Nightsish than anywhere I've seen in Arabia... Does it actually feel like that when you are there?"

"Very much so. It's a really exciting country and so beautiful. It's got everything... mountains, desert, beautiful architecture, history, greenery, beaches... It gets a bit hot in Marrakech in the summer, but only for two or three months. I wasn't there for a whole year, so I can't say what it's like in mid-winter, but I gather it can be pretty nippy."

"Why did you leave?"

"I only went there in the first place because there was an emergency and I happened to be available. I'd been expecting to go to Turin but there was a mix-up and I lost out. Still, I was happy when things turned out the way they did. In many ways I'd like to have stayed longer but the pay was dreadful - Morocco's a poor country - and we had to work incredibly long hours so when Global offered me a job in Athens I accepted it... and I stayed there for a couple of years."

*   *   *   *

Within a few days Julian decided that he was happy in Khajal.

"It's true that it's not much to look at," he said to his colleagues. "The town is a chaotic mess and it has none of the charm of the Moroccan medinas with their exotic souqs and mazes of tangled alleys. The country - from what I've seen of it so far - is flat and boring. Even the famous dunes where we had our picnic this weekend are nothing to write home about - just heaps of sand plonked haphazardly here and there on a rubbly desert floor as if they don't belong there at all. But I really like the Khajalis I've met. I find our students gracious and friendly - even the middle-aged conservative ones - and they are interesting, intelligent and amusing. I can't understand how the people at Head Office could have been so wrong about them. At the briefing they gave me when they first decided to send me here I was told the Khajalis were okay to deal with on the whole but as thick as two short planks."

"Did Tom Pryke tell you that?" Peter asked.

"He and their other old Middle East hand whose name I didn't catch... Well actually, I think I did catch it but I've forgotten it."

The trainees (with one or two exceptions) took an immediate liking to Julian and within days he and a rather louche mechanic from the Marine Department called Khamis had become firm friends. On the surface they appeared to have little in common. Khamis was a passionate supporter of Khajal's al Nasr football club and Real Madrid and, although he was pushing thirty-five, he still played occasionally in his own local neighbourhood team. Julian had no interest in any kind of sports and was a keen birdwatcher – an activity that Khamis dismissed as unworthy of a sane adult, though he made allowances for Julian as an eccentric Englishman.

However, there was one thing they did share in common. For all his diffidence and apparent naivety, Julian was unusually streetwise in his ability to detect a fellow devotee of the weed. Perhaps Khamis had a particular look that he recognized from kindred spirits in Morocco, or maybe – consciously or unconsciously – he dropped an occasional hint or double-entendre that Julian was able to pick up and interpret. Julian was probably easier for Khamis to identify because he was by nature somewhat transparent, not to say indiscreet.

Anyway, however the signals were exchanged, within three weeks of their first meeting they were regularly getting stoned together. Khamis had a Pakistani friend from the North-West Frontier Province who supplied him and many of the local potheads so they were never short of what Julian liked to call "the wherewithal".

Their sessions took place at least twice a week at one or other of the many isolated seaside spots outside the town that were accessible by car. Usually it was just the two of them, though occasionally they were joined by a couple of Khamis's friends. They never smoked in each other's houses. Khamis was determined that his wife's blissful ignorance of her husband's "taste for the exotic" (another quote from Julian) should continue for the rest of their happily married lives, while Edward's clear disapproval of such practices was almost as strong as his fear of the Law (which was considerable) and Julian was determined to preserve the harmony of their life in the villa.

Over the following few weeks the Mottled Oil teachers received periodic bulletins on Monotone from London, though not from their old boss. Now that Khajal was no longer available to finance his schemes and help pay his rent, Freddy saw no reason to take any further interest in his former branch or its employees (He had many qualities, some laudable, but sentiment was not one of them). The only remaining link between Monotone and Khajal was through Roy, who was now working on an English language course for beginner to pre-advanced level students that Freddy planned to market as Monotone's answer to Robert Strawmaker's *Global English* series.

A month and a half into his new job he was still waiting for his first salary, which would have been modest even on paper, though just about enough to house, feed and clothe a single teetotal Londoner with simple tastes. Roy was not a teetotaller, his tastes ran to the mildly expensive and, although he was single, he and his girlfriend were hoping to marry in the near future. Since returning to London he had been living on his savings from the years he had spent at Mottled Oil but he was aware that he could not continue to do so indefinitely.

Edward had kept in touch with Mike Kelly, who was living with his sister in Northampton after a short stay in hospital. Although there was no chance that his eyesight would ever recover, his organ damage turned out not to be as severe as originally feared and, according to his doctors, the chances were that, all being well, he would eventually be able to live a more or less normal life.

"I gather my liver (or is it my spleen?) is still not a hundred per cent but it seems to be better and the hope is that it will continue to improve," he wrote. "I'm also getting used to having only half my previous field of vision and my brain has started to adjust to it. Obviously I won't be able to drive a car again or do anything like that, but I can read and watch television. I can get about too, but I'm still on crutches and I have to have regular physio sessions."

Back in Khajal, the salary review turned out to be relatively painless. The twenty per cent pay rise was scrapped and the teachers were offered an eight per cent increase instead – twelve per cent down from the previous level but still reasonably attractive. Everyone, including Peter, agreed that this was acceptable and they all signed contracts with their new employer.

The school flourished in a modest way. After an intensive advertising campaign in the local press its student intake grew significantly (though not dramatically) and another local British expatriate housewife called Pearl was recruited to take on the extra English classes.

A Khajali friend of Steve's who taught at one of the government primary schools volunteered his services as a TAFL (Teaching Arabic as a Foreign Language) teacher and the head of Arabic at Global Schools (Middle East) came over to give him a crash course in teaching basic conversational Gulf Arabic to foreigners. Nick ran the school competently with Jean's and Pearl's assistance. The plan to bring out "a full-time principal, director or whatever" was put on hold but not dropped altogether.

Changes were taking place elsewhere too. After several weeks of rumours the government announced it was nationalising the country's oil industry and that with effect from May 1st Mottled Oil would have a new name – the Khajal National Petroleum Company, or KNPC. Under a new agreement Mottled would continue to run the production, administration and marketing side, but for a fixed fee, while the Khajali government would own

KNPC's assets and receive the proceeds from its sales.

There would be few immediately noticeable changes. Most of the employees would remain in their present jobs, but there would now be a Khajali chairman – Hussain Abbas al Marri, formerly tea boy, clerk, Personnel Officer, Personnel Affairs Supervisor and lately Assistant Personnel Manager at Mottled Oil. He was not popular with either his peers or his underlings, but in the kind of circles in which he moved popularity was not considered an asset and - or so his old colleagues claimed - being almost universally disliked was probably one of the qualifications that got him the job ("Not much danger of cronyism there because he hasn't got any cronies").

"The good thing is that he won't actually be able to do very much," said Edward's and Mike's friend Salim, formerly a technical trainee, now an admin assistant in the Finance Department. "The real power is in the hands of the Managing Director (and the government of course), though it'll be the Chairman who has the nice big office with pile carpets and lots of telephones and we'll probably see him every day in the papers and on TV as the public face of KNPC. And it's just as well that he will be merely a figurehead. He is a thoroughly nasty character and if he was given free rein to throw his weight around as he pleased there is no knowing what he might do."

In June the life of Global Schools (Khajal) took a dramatic turn.

"In a way I suppose it's a bit of a relief to know it's not just Monotone that has scandals but I must say I wasn't expecting this," Steve said.

The "this" he was referring to was as follows. For several months Khamis's Pakistani friend (let's call him X, not for the sake of anonymity but because he had rather a long and complicated name) had been expanding his customer base and the scale of his activities grew to a point where it was inevitable word would eventually reach the authorities.

He became increasingly careless and when an undercover policeman approached him with a request for half a Kilo of hashish - for which he offered to pay considerably more than the going market rate - X leapt at the opportunity. He was arrested as he was in the process of delivering the goods and, during the course of his interrogation, he was promised a reduction in his prison sentence if he gave the CID the names of his regular customers. The list included Khamis and the police put him under surveillance.

Khamis and Julian were aware of X's arrest and its possible consequences but, as Khamis said: "We've just bought our regular monthly supply and it would be a crime to throw it away. And after all, we don't know when we are going to find a reliable new replacement for X".

"We should be all right as long as we're reasonably discreet," Julian agreed. "Which means it might be better if we just have one session a week for the time being."

Late one evening about a fortnight after X was arrested, Khamis and Julian were driving back into town when a weather-beaten Peugeot saloon car swerved across the road in front of them and stopped and a man in Khajali dress got out and came towards them.

"God! Are we being hijacked?" Julian said.

The man tapped on the driver's window and produced a CID card.

"I'd like you to come with me to the police station," he said.

"Why? What's the problem?" Khamis said.

"Just follow me to the police station and everything will be explained to you."

At the police station, a constable and a sniffer dog examined the car and Julian and Khamis were ordered to turn out their pockets in the interrogation room. They and the car appeared to be in the clear until the dog started to show an unusual interest in the car's gear stick. The constable removed the cap from the knob handle and found a small quantity of hashish inside about the size of a hazelnut.

"Ha!" he cried triumphantly and put it in his plastic evidence pouch before handing it over to the officer in charge.

"Found in your car Khamis. Any comment?" the officer inquired.

"Nothing to do with me," Khamis replied. "If it really was in my car as you claim, somebody else must have put it there."

"Like who?"

"Maybe one of the people when I took it in for a service. Or someone at the car wash when I left it there. I'm not the only person who has had access to it."

A doctor was brought and blood samples were taken from the two suspects. The results came back positive.

"Of course it was your hashish. It's ridiculous to say that you don't know anything about it," the officer said. "But even if it wasn't yours, we now know for certain that you have both been smoking cannabis of one kind or another, so it's lock-up for the two of you tonight. I might remind you, though, before we start to ask any more questions, that it would be much better for you to tell the truth. Even if you don't we'll get to the truth anyway and if you lie it will be the worse for you. Judges don't like drug users anyway but they're especially tough on them if they are liars as well."

*   *   *   *

When Edward got up the next morning he was surprised and a little concerned to find that Julian's bed had not been slept in, but it was only when he arrived at the Training Centre – slightly late because he was not due in class till the second lesson - that he discovered what had happened. The first people he saw were George Weever and Nick - Weever looking grim and angry and

Nick uncharacteristically ill at ease. He wished them a polite good morning and turned to Nick.

"I was just going to call you," he said. "Do you know anything about what's happened to Julian? He didn't come home last night."

"That's why we're here," Weever said gruffly. "Your senior teacher's been arrested..."

"Arrested?!"

"Yes... Not a good start for Global." Weever looked meaningfully at Nick, who cringed visibly.

"Is it something serious?" Edward asked.

"Serious? You can say that again. It's drugs. When we signed up with Global we thought... a new broom... no more cock-ups... And now this has happened. And he is your man, not Monotone's, isn't he?" He looked accusingly at Nick.

"Honestly, George. I just don't know what to say," Nick replied.

"Well, let's go to my office and try to get an update from the police and see if there's anything we can do to salvage the situation."

They left and Edward joined his shell-shocked colleagues in the teacher's room.

"In a way I suppose it's a bit of a relief to know it's not just Monotone that has scandals but I must say I wasn't expecting this," Steve said.

*   *   *   *

Under the previous colonial system there were British courts in the Gulf as well as local ones and British lawbreakers were tried in them. And although by the late 1970s several years had passed since the country had become independent, something of the old mentality and practices still survived in the minds of the Khajali authorities. This was why, following Julian's arrest, the Ministry of the Interior responded by suspending its normal policy of "Let the

Law take its course" because, they said: "He's British and that means we've got a problem. What are we going to do about him? There aren't any British courts here anymore but it might be embarrassing if we tried him for a major offence in a Khajali criminal court."

The British Embassy had no sympathy for Julian but they were bound to support him as a British subject in trouble abroad and they saw his case as an interesting challenge. Their legal expert was optimistic.

"Of course it will really depend on what line the Khajalis decide to take," he said. "But the thing in his favour is that nothing was found on his person and he wasn't the owner of the car..."

"But his blood test was positive," the consul said.

"Yes indeed. But perhaps it could be argued that it was his proximity to a hashish smoker that caused the positive test result. He wasn't smoking anything but the smoke from his friend's cigarette wafted up his nostrils – all unbeknownst to him, since he had no idea his friend wasn't smoking ordinary tobacco. In other words, he was a passive hashish smoker and he just happened to be in the wrong place at the wrong time."

"I can't believe the medical evidence would support that theory. After all, they were outside in the open air. Still, it could be worth a try if you think the authorities might decide it would solve the problem of what to do with this pesky Englishman."

The British ambassador agreed to suggest it at his next audience with the Emir. The Emir was amused and approved it, provided that the case was seen to be dealt with "through the proper legal channels".

On his next consular visit the vice-consul briefed Julian on the plan and told him that this was the story he should sign in his statement. (As yet, nothing had been signed, although there had been several inconclusive interrogation sessions at which both Julian and Khamis protested their innocence and questioned the validity of the blood tests.)

"I'm sorry but I'm not going to land Khamis in it just to save my own skin," Julian said.

"You'd bloody well better," the vice-consul said. "Look here, my lad, you've got to do what we tell you. Otherwise you won't get any more help from us."

"Well at least let me speak to Khamis first and see what he says."

"OK. Fair enough."

To Julian's surprise, Khamis was in favour of the plan.

"It's obvious that our protestations of innocence aren't going anywhere, but that's not the point," he whispered. (The constable on duty was out of earshot but they wanted to be absolutely sure that nobody else could hear their conversation.) "If I'm the only one of us found guilty I'm not going to get a longer sentence just because you are found not guilty. Actually, it would probably win me some public sympathy and that could sway the court slightly. I also have a strong *waasta* (influential connection). Several in fact. My brother works in the Prime Minister's office and I have a cousin who is second in charge of protocol at the Palace, so when the Emir announces an amnesty for convicted offenders – as he usually does to mark the month of Ramadan – my name will almost certainly be on his list ... The only thing that really worries me at the moment is what my wife is going to say about all this. It's bound to have come as a severe shock to her."

Khamis's predictions proved to be mainly correct and the case ended satisfactorily for all concerned. He was released a few months later in time to celebrate the end of Ramadan with his family (who were delighted and relieved to have him back with them) and he returned to his old job in the Marine Department. Julian was found not guilty but deported as an undesirable alien and Global found a squeaky-clean replacement for him at KNPC, though it was a while before they were able to restore their tarnished reputation.

9.

THE OTHER END OF MONOTONE

From Roy's journal

NOTE. Keeping a journal isn't really my thing and the only reason I'm doing it now is because I suspect the coming weeks could be a crucial period in the life of Monotone and worth recording for posterity.

10th May 1978

Until late 1975 Monotone London was really quite a small operation – just a head office and an English language institute with a couple of classrooms in a run-down building near King's Cross. Then after Monotone Beirut was destroyed, Freddy moved the Arabic school to London and rented a three-storey house in Kensington, which is where we're all based at present. I think it's a Regency building but I'm no expert so I wouldn't swear to it. It looks quite majestic - cream stucco with steps leading up to the front door and a pair of columns on either side of the porch. The offices are on the top floor and the classrooms are on the two lower floors.

I've been back in England for a little over three weeks now. Freddy has decided that the time has finally come for us to write our own English courses and I agree with him. After all, Monotone has been in this game for a couple of decades - not quite as long as Global but certainly long enough to have accumulated a fair bit of experience and expertise. I myself have been teaching English at various levels to Arab students for nearly ten years - in Khajal, Libya and Saudi Arabia - and our branches in the Gulf have produced tons of material. Of course, much of it has been ephemeral stuff and found its way into the nearest waste-paper basket after an outing or two, but a lot of it is reusable and some of it is very good.

Anyway, Freddy has appointed me as his chief course writer and he has promised to pay me a salary. It would be quite a comfortable one if I was living in Khajal but London is frighteningly expensive and I'm not too sure how I'm going to manage on it here. I have my savings from my years at Mottled Oil, but I really don't want to squander them on subsidising my lifestyle in England - not long-term anyway, though two or three months probably wouldn't hurt too much.

Although I've visited London every year since I was a child, living here feels strange after a decade in the Gulf and North Africa. Actually, I suppose I would have found it strange anyway because until this month I don't think I've ever spent more than two or three nights in this city at any one time, even though I grew up only just over an hour away by train from Marylebone (in Buckinghamshire, if you readers are interested).

It wasn't my choice to return to England as soon as this, but here I am and being back in my homeland does have its compensations. For one thing, I am at last beginning to feel that my "real life" has finally begun. For an expatriate like me on a bachelor contract, living in Khajal was in some ways like existing in a vacuum if you get what I mean. Perhaps that's not a very good way to describe it; what I'm trying to say is that it was a bit like spending your life in a sort of waiting room where everything is on hold including career, as well as serious long-term personal relationships.

Before I left England to work abroad all those years ago, my idea was to get a well-paid job in the Gulf for two or three years until I had made enough money for my then girlfriend Susie and me to get married and set up house. The plan was that she would stay in England; she already had a budding career as a journalist and the job opportunities for expatriate women would have been fairly limited in the region where I was thinking of going. Then at the end of my stint I would come home, pockets bulging with cash, and move on to the next stage of my life - becoming a married man and embarking on a steady career with prospects.

Things didn't turn out that way. After about eighteen months Susie got tired of waiting and found someone else (or perhaps she just decided on reflection that I wasn't the man for her) and I began to feel that I had no particular reason to return home. I don't know why, but in my mind I had lumped Susie, marriage and career together as one package, so when Susie dumped me the rest of the plan fell apart. In the meantime, I was beginning to realise that teaching English as a foreign language (or "TEFL", as we TEFL teachers call it) was a perfectly respectable occupation in its own right. I had discovered I was good at it and it gave me all the job satisfaction I wanted.

In the summer holiday after Susie and I broke up, I ran into Helen - a girl I had been friendly with at university though we hadn't known one another well - and during the remaining three weeks of my leave we saw quite a lot of each other. Over the next few years we became close friends, but it was only about two years ago that we started to talk about the possibility of marriage. I won't go into detail about how we eventually came to the conclusion it would be a good idea (at least in principle).

Anyway, that's the situation at present, and the fact that I'm now back in England, probably for good, means that a wedding in the near future is a distinct possibility. Helen and I have already started talking - tentatively - about dates.

14ᵗʰ May 1978

Freddy is unbelievably frustrating to work with.

I had more than an inkling of this when I was his humble employee in Khajal, but now he and I are sitting in adjacent offices in London and I sometimes feel I could scream. Every day he has a new scheme which he invariably describes as a guaranteed money-spinner, only to drop it a few days later. ("I don't know why we have been wasting time on this business English with ballroom dancing plan for Japanese executives in dreary old London. Skiing in Switzerland and afternoon lessons in conversational French is a much better combination and would appeal to a far wider public... I must get onto my friend Gustave in Montreux and see what he thinks.")

And I'm only talking about the four weeks or so since I joined Monotone London. I wouldn't care about it all that much if it wasn't likely to affect me personally, but he's so fickle that I'm worried the Monotone English course may end up in the bin too as a victim of his next bright idea.

*   *   *   *

When I was still in charge of Monotone Khajal, Freddy rang me with an urgent demand for money because, he said, the bailiffs were about to turn up and seize their office equipment. I believed him at the time but later, after discussing it with Edward (my predecessor as branch manager out there), I decided it was just a ploy. Now I'm beginning to suspect he was probably telling the truth after all.

Yesterday afternoon we had a visit from the estate agent who rents us our office here and he handed Freddy a very legal-looking letter threatening us with eviction because our rent is nearly three months overdue, which puts us seriously in breach of our lease agreement.

Now that Freddy no longer has the Khajal account to plunder, he has started putting pressure on the other branches, though none of them have anything like the kind of income we used to have with the Mottled Oil contract and they find it hard enough just sending him their monthly remittances. The infuriating thing is that several of Freddy's ideas are genuinely good (I don't mean the two examples I've just mentioned!) and I think they would succeed if he gave them the chance to get off the ground.

3rd June 1978

Freddy's wife Lucinda is the first to arrive in the morning and it is her task to unlock the front door and let us in. Twice over the past week she has turned up without the key and the staff and students have had to sit around for an hour in the Bellissima Cafe next door while she makes the return trip between our Monotone office in Kensington and the family's home in Maida Vale to collect it.

This morning - the second time she forgot the key - she was effusively apologetic though Shawqi, our Saudi Proficiency Level student, told her not to get upset about it as "these things happen to the best of us, *even* me". He said this with a straight face because has an exceptionally high opinion of himself.

"I'm always forgetting things," he said. "Just before we left Jeddah to come here to England I mislaid our tickets and do you know what my wife said to me?" He began to giggle.

"No Shawqi. What did she say?"

"She said 'It's lucky your genitals aren't detachable. If they were, we'd never have been able to have any children'".

He slapped his thigh and chortled merrily. Lucinda blushed as she is a bit prudish.

Freddy was less amused by Lucinda's memory lapse. In fact he is quite snappy with her these days. I may be imagining it, but I have a suspicion that the stresses of the past few months could be putting their marriage under strain. The atmosphere at work has generally been rather glum since I moved here, though of course I've got nothing else to compare it with as Freddy has always been my distant boss in a faraway land and I've never worked in the same building with him before.

In fact there have been times over the past few days when I've thought he looks seriously depressed.

From afar I always pictured Freddy as a man of action rather than a contemplative type - a mercurial character whose thoughts and feelings changed like the shake of a kaleidoscope from one moment to the next so that he never had time to be depressed. I am sure he can't be suffering from clinical depression, which is a perpetual state of mind. His present mood is far more likely to be just worry brought on by Monotone's money problems and I'm certain that if a few thousand pounds landed in his current account tomorrow he would be as right as rain in a flash.

20th June 1978

I haven't been paid a penny since I started working here but Freddy has promised he'll be able to give me something "very soon". He has been absent for the past couple of days - "a slight stomach upset", according to Lucinda, who is holding the fort. (When I say "holding the fort", I hope the reader won't get the impression that we are under siege - that is not quite how I feel(!) - so perhaps my choice of words here is infelicitous. Anyway, I expect you know what I mean.)

You would have thought that being at Head Office I would have some idea about what is going on, but over these past few weeks my colleagues and I have all been equally in the dark. There are eight of us apart from Freddy and Lucinda: the Arabic teachers Mazin, Farouq and Jirjis (Mazin is Palestinian and Farouq and Jirjis are from Lebanon); the English teachers Louisa, Sally and me; Marcel - the French teacher; and Padmini - the secretary, receptionist and school manager who looks about fifteen but must be in her early twenties.

At present we have six Arabic classes including a five-week intensive course for businessmen, eight English classes at various levels (I am teaching elementary for two hours a day in the early afternoon and spend the rest of the day trying to put a course together upstairs), and three French classes (one elementary, one intermediate and one advanced; all Marcel's students are native English speakers).

We all (my seven colleagues and I) get on extremely well together and after work Jirjis, Louisa, Sally, Marcel and I usually sit in the Bellissima Cafe for an hour or so and end up speculating about our situation. We know that things are looking uncertain at the moment but we have no solid information about whether they are really as bad as we suspect they might be.

3rd July 1978

For the past week Freddy and Lucinda have been spending most of the day closeted in Freddy's office with the door locked.

"Most disconcerting," Padmini says. "The students are getting worried now. They can sense that something is wrong but at the moment I'm the only face of Monotone they can deal with apart from their teachers, and I can't tell them anything because I don't know any more than they do... The only definite thing I've noticed recently is that Freddy (or possibly Lucinda) is spending a lot of time on the telephone. Their line is almost constantly engaged."

8th July 1978

We all turned up for work at the usual time this morning but the office was locked and there was no sign of either Lucinda or Freddy (They usually come in together when Freddy is in London).

"They must have overslept," we decided. We stuck a notice on the door to say where we were and repaired to the Bellissima for coffee with some of our students. More joined us a few minutes later. After half an hour we returned to the office. It was still locked.

"Has anyone got their home number?" I asked.

"I have. I'll see if I can get hold of them," Padmini said.

There was no answer from the Maida Vale house, so we decided to put a larger notice on the door of the Monotone building referring any callers to the Bellissima, where one of us would be on duty and ready to explain to them that the school was closed and our employers' current whereabouts were unknown. We agreed to take one-hour shifts at the cafe through the morning or until Lucinda or Freddy arrived. The Bellissima manager was sympathetic and told us that although he was (in his words) "a hard-headed businessman", on this occasion he would not expect his Monotone regulars to drink more coffee (or eat more cake) than their stomachs were comfortable with. In other words, he allowed us to sit at his tables without running up a bill.

9th July 1978

Neither Freddy nor Lucinda put in an appearance yesterday but Mr. Orhan, the estate agent, arrived at around lunch time, saw the notice on the front door and caught me at the Bellissima just as I was about to go off shift. We have seen him at the office several times over the past two months, but previously we ordinary staff members have not been involved in administrative matters like the office rent.

Yesterday was different. He told me that "Mr. Frederick Barnes" (Freddy) had been served with an order to attend a tribunal hearing that morning for non-payment of rent, but that he had failed to turn up and the panel had ruled in favour of the landlords. Consequently, and under the terms of the lease, Monotone could now be evicted immediately.

"I wish I could help you but we have no idea where he is. He seems to have disappeared off the face of the earth and the first we knew about it was when we arrived for work at 9 o'clock this morning and found the door locked," I said.

"Then it looks like we'll have to force our way in... well, not exactly force our way in - unless he's changed the lock - because we've got a key to the front door," Mr. Orhan said. "Perhaps one of you could come along tomorrow morning to witness my entry and confirm that I'm not a burglar... that is, if any curious bystander should happen to ask."

We exchanged telephone numbers. Then he left and I went back to my bedsit in Shepherd's Bush and called Padmini to keep her in the picture. As we are bereft of our management at the moment, she is the nearest thing to a person in charge.

It may appear to the outside world that we are taking things in our stride - none of us has had hysterics yet or burst into tears in public at the prospect of imminent unemployment - but I know we are all extremely worried and upset. Last night I lay in bed for hours trying to get to sleep and thinking dark thoughts about Freddy as I blamed him for my insomnia.

"If he's not ill or languishing in a dungeon somewhere - which is most unlikely - the only other possibility is that he has gone to ground... or perhaps left the country. Whatever he's up to, he's clearly trying to dodge his creditors. And he obviously doesn't give a damn about his staff... In fact, when I next see him - I assume I will see him again one day - I'm going to give him a piece of my mind... And... And... And... And I'll tear him off a strip too," I thought to myself, grinding my teeth as I tossed and turned fretfully between the sheets. "Or perhaps I'll punch him on the nose" (Actually, I am not a violent person, so I probably wouldn't go that far, though I fear pieces of mind and tearing off strips would be unlikely to affect him much; his conscience is impervious to rebuke).

To my amazement, an opportunity to do one of those things arose almost immediately when Freddy suddenly appeared before me dressed in cricket whites and a Panama hat with a fatuous grin on his face. I was walking along the Brompton Road towards South Kensington and he was approaching from the opposite direction.

"Hello Roy," he called cheerily, waving a scarlet handkerchief in my direction. "Come and have an ice-cream."

"Now look here, Freddy," I said. "This..."

I was about to say "This just isn't good enough", but at the sound of my own voice I woke up, deeply frustrated and furious at having been cut off before I could tell him what I thought of him. The mood lasted until sleep finally returned as the dawn chorus was beginning.

10th July 1978

This morning Padmini and I met Mr. Orhan, by appointment, outside the Monotone office in Kensington. He found that his key could still open the front door so he entered the building and walked round the premises, peering into each room and tutting to himself (unjustifiably in my opinion; the place is beautifully clean and tidy; in that regard Monotone are model tenants) while we trailed along behind him. When he left he stuck an official-looking notice on the door announcing that "Sheringham Estate and Letting Agents" had retaken possession of the property. We are wondering what is going to happen to the furniture and contents.

None of us has heard a word from Freddy or Lucinda. We all met up at the Bellissima again this morning and exchanged ideas - inconclusively - on what to do next. Things are really rather critical for us at the moment as all the personnel files - including contracts, qualification certificates, PAYE cards etc. - are locked up in the filing cabinet in Freddy's office.

I wonder if Freddy has been in touch with any of the Monotone branches in the Gulf. One of us should ring them and see if there is any news.

12th July 1978

The Kuwait branch has had a call from Freddy asking for money to be sent to a bank in Paris. This doesn't necessarily mean that he's living in France. However, I think it might help us to trace him, though banks are famously reluctant to disclose details about their clients, even to the police (I know this for a fact because I watch a lot of TV crime serials).

Padmini says she has the telephone numbers of Freddy's solicitor and accountant. Surely they would be prepared to tell us what they know if we explained our situation to them?

13th July 1978

Mr. Watkins, Monotone's accountant, was flabbergasted when

Padmini called him this morning and told him what had happened. According to him, for the past few months our money situation has been - "let's be blunt - pretty bad", but at their last meeting about ten days ago Freddy insisted everything was going to be fine and the only down side was the current cash-flow problem which would be resolved very soon.

I always thought "cash-flow problem" was a euphemism for going broke, but according to Mr. Watkins it does not have to mean that, and from what I recall from some of my telephone conversations with him when I was branch manager in Khajal, Freddy has a fairly laid-back attitude towards it.

"Calling a temporary cash-flow hiatus a problem means you are turning a perfectly commonplace state of affairs into a melodrama," he told me (I'm not quoting him verbatim but this is the gist of what he said). "We should really see it as a minor administrative matter - not a particularly good thing but not actually something you could describe as a problem either. In human terms - if you want to compare it with everyday ailments - it would probably be somewhere between hiccups and a cold".

According to Mr. Watkins, Freddy never gave him the slightest hint about his plans to abscond. "Though as far as I can see it doesn't look as if he is actually doing anything illegal," he told Padmini. "Not yet anyway. But from a moral point of view his behaviour is unforgivable unless he has a really good explanation for it." He has promised to keep us "in the loop".

Padmini has also been in touch with Brenda Stiff, Freddy's solicitor. She was surprised by the news too but refused to be drawn on whether she considered Freddy's sudden departure "acceptable" or not. However, she will also keep us posted - with the proviso that any information she gives us must not entail "breaking lawyer-client confidentiality".

We have all started thinking about looking for new jobs. My

English-teaching colleagues are living more or less hand to mouth, so for them unemployment is a luxury they can ill afford. Mazin, Farouq and Jirjis give private tuition to well-heeled businessmen in the evenings, which is well paid but probably not enough to live on without the income from their day jobs. Still, they're unlikely to be job-hunting for long because there is strong demand for Arabic in the London business community.

Marcel seems more amused than worried. I think he regards his job as an agreeable hobby rather than an essential means of keeping body and soul together, though he doesn't fancy the prospect of unemployment either.

17th July 1978

Freddy has surfaced in Paris. Yesterday he called Mr. Watkins from there to check whether, as a UK resident, he could open a bank account in France without getting into "complications" with the Inland Revenue. Mr. Watkins passed his contact details to Padmini, who spoke to him last night. When he heard her voice he sounded cornered and a little taken aback and began giving her a rambling justification of his conduct. After a few minutes of this Padmini interrupted him sharply.

"That wasn't what I rang you about," she said. "The first thing we need to do is get into your filing cabinet so that we can retrieve our personnel stuff. I don't know if you realise it, but we are in limbo at the moment. Our salaries have not been paid this month... we don't know when or if they ever will be... and the Arabic teachers tell me they can't even sign up for new jobs unless they have the right paperwork."

"I quite understand, Padmini dear," he replied soothingly. "I'm sorry I wasn't able to give you more notice, but as I was starting to tell you just now before you interrupted me, a fantastic opportunity has suddenly come up here which will solve all our money headaches and that's why I had to travel to Paris in a hurry. But don't worry. I should be back in London quite soon."

"But what about in the meantime? We haven't got an office or a school and we can't just sit around waiting. Could you at least authorise us to break into your personnel drawer so that we can get our papers. We're all unemployed at the moment..."

"Don't say that, Padmini. In my eyes you are still my much-valued employees and you always will be."

"That's as may be, but we've got to eat. Please call your lawyer and tell her you are allowing us access to our files. I don't know what the legal procedures are but I imagine she will have to be present when we break the lock. Or has somebody else got a second key?"

"Lucinda has but she is with me in Paris."

"I'll go and see Ms. Stiff first thing tomorrow morning and alert her to be ready to receive your call imminently. Is that OK?"

I am hopeful that Freddy will do what he is told. Padmini is a forceful young woman when she goes on the attack and if I was him I certainly would not care to be on the receiving end.

23rd July 1978

It took a couple more calls from Padmini before Freddy finally got round to giving Brenda Stiff some kind of power of attorney. I don't think Mr. Orhan is sequestrating the office contents - certainly not all of them anyway - and he was quite happy to let us into the building with Ms. Stiff today. Now that we have retrieved our stuff, I think we can say that our relationship with Monotone has come to an end. I would be surprised if Freddy returned to London in the foreseeable future as I gather several rather determined people would want to see him if he did.

A few days ago I toyed with the idea of suing him for non-payment of salary, but I don't think there would be any point because his financial situation at the moment is probably even worse than mine. And although I resent the way we have been treated, I don't actually dislike him and I have no desire to add to his problems just for the sake of it.

25th July 1978

I think it is called serendipity. It looks as if I may have just had the most extraordinary stroke of good fortune. Or perhaps not. Plenty of things could go wrong between now and the final outcome, and even if it is as promising as it seems it puts me in a bit of a dilemma. A couple of nights ago my father rang me on the communal telephone here at my lodgings to say that my old colleague Edward was trying to get in touch with me, and yesterday morning I managed to get hold of him at Mottled Oil's training centre. News of Monotone's demise had not reached Khajal so the first thing he said to me was:

"How are you enjoying your new job?"

"Well, actually I haven't got one," I replied and explained that Monotone had ceased to exist ("unless it manages to come back from the dead"). International calls are expensive so I didn't go into detail.

"So you are currently unemployed. Well, that's a bit of luck," he said. "How do you feel about coming back here as senior teacher?"

"But you've already got one. Has Julian decided he doesn't want to stay in Khajal?"

"He's been deported. I won't give you the full story but I know for a fact - well, almost for a fact - that Global would be happy to take you on as his replacement if you want the job."

"Well it would be great if I could come back. Though I've sort of got engaged to an old friend called Helen here in England so I'll have to discuss it with her before I can give you a definite answer. Have you sounded out Global yet?"

"Not Global in London, but our branch manager Nick Hoskins... remember him? Nick says he would strongly recommend you on the basis of your past reputation as a teacher and he can't see any reason why they should turn you down."

28th July 1978

Over the weekend Helen and I talked long into the night. She is in favour of my taking the job, so I'm going to go ahead and tell Nick that I'm ready and willing to start more or less immediately. The question now is what Helen is going to do. She is a qualified architect and I know she would be highly employable in Khajal because there has been a massive building boom there since the price of oil went through the roof and their oil industry was nationalised.

She says she would like the experience of working abroad, but she has some reservations about leaving CWA - her present employers. They like her and she likes them and if she stays with them it is quite likely she will end up as a partner one day. Though as she wouldn't expect us to live in Khajal for more than a few years at most, she is hoping they might agree to give her a sort of extended sabbatical (I am sure that is not the right term, but she would like to think they would keep a position open for her to return to).

Another possibility is if CWA were to send her to Khajal to work for them. They have put in a bid for a big construction project in New Khajal City and she understands the odds in favour of their getting the contract are between quite good and very good.

She wouldn't be able to come out to Khajal with me for a number of reasons. For one thing, I shall probably be expected to travel within the next ten days and CWA would not look too kindly upon her if she left without giving them fair notice. In any case, the Khajali authorities would refuse to give a residence permit to an unemployed single woman, even if - or particularly if (!) - she told them she was moving in with me. They probably wouldn't object if she was a resident with a work visa and we lived together discreetly, but unmarried couples are not recognised under Khajali law. And even if things could be arranged so that she was able to leave CWA immediately, my understanding is that under English law it would not be possible for us to get married here before I leave because the powers that be would need a few weeks' notice (I don't know if Gretna Green would still be an option but I suspect it wouldn't).

In the end we decided that (*Global volente*) I shall go out to Khajal next week and she will stay in London. She will discuss her situation with her bosses at CWA and in a few months' time I will take a week's unpaid leave and return to England so that we can marry and travel back to Khajal together (or not, if she decides to stay in her present job). Alternatively, if CWA send her to Khajal as their employee we can get married at the British Embassy there. In the meantime, I will try to persuade Global to agree to give me married accommodation or a housing allowance (though of course if CWA win the New Khajal City contract and send her out to work on their project, they will almost certainly house her handsomely in their own accommodation and I will move in there with her).

1st August 1978

Hurrah! I signed a contract at Global's head office this morning and I'm booked to fly out in four days' time. Bye bye London.

10.

DEJA VU

It was a late autumn afternoon in the year 1978 and the end of another working day at Khajal National Petroleum Company (KNPC). The siren had just sounded and the four o'clock exodus had begun.

However, there was no sign of movement in the car park outside the main administration building at the top of the hill. Up here too there was a daily ritual, but it was not regulated by the siren. Within the next few minutes, some forty pairs of eyes would take up position behind the tinted windows of their offices and gaze expectantly towards the Deputy Managing Director's Range Rover, willing it to join the queue of cars that were heading towards the exit gate. His departure would be the signal for his underlings to put away their files, cover their typewriters, pack their handbags and briefcases and set off for home, confident in the knowledge that their reputations for diligence were still untarnished.

Meanwhile, a couple of hundred yards down the road the staff of the Personnel Department had gathered at the Sports and Social Centre's Sheikh Jassim Banqueting Hall (formerly the Small Party Room), where they were perched awkwardly on high-back sofas and trying their hardest to chat to each other in a relaxed and natural manner. Normally they too would be up at the main office peering out of their windows like the rest of their colleagues, but today they had abandoned their posts with clear consciences while the boss was still at work because they had been summoned to attend a Farewell-to-One-of-Our Colleagues Tea Party - a long-established tradition dating from the Company's Mottled Oil days.

The only Khajalis among them were Majid al Khulaifi and Rashid al Khater. The others were mainly expatriate Indians or Northern Arabs. Violet de Souza, Felicia Alvarez, Tulip Lamond, Lavender O'Connor and Marie-Antoinette Williams were typists from Bombay, Sabri Abd al Rabbo, Samir Touqan, Mahmoud Anani and Anis Selous were Palestinian intermediate level staff and Richard Pollard, Roy Sladen, Andrew Watson, Steve Kettle and the guest of honour were English teachers subcontracted from Global Schools (Khajal). With the exception of two of the English contingent and Majid and Rashid, who were barely out of their teens and had recently finished their clerical training, they had all worked with the Company during the days when it was part of the vast multinational Mottled Oil empire. They knew each other well and in normal circumstances relations between them - both in and out of work - were generally easy and casual.

However, the Farewell Tea Party was different and there was a degree of tension in the air. Although they were expected to treat it as an informal get-together, they all recognized it for what it really was - a semi-official extension of work. Consequently, the dilemma of "Should we still regard each other as official work colleagues or are we supposed to be socialising as friends?" had put a strain on the gathering, and while there were beaming smiles in abundance, they had something of the rictus about them and conversation was nervous and stilted. Edward Holdsworth, the guest of honour, was the most nervous of all because he knew he would soon have to address a few words to the gathering and, while he was always quite comfortable in a classroom full of trainees, he was terrified of speaking in public. A skinny man in his early thirties with thinning hair, he sat slightly hunched, inspecting his fingernails and glancing uneasily from time to time at the faded curtains and the Chinese nylon carpet with its pattern of pink and yellow peonies.

The hydraulic doors wheezed open and a hush fell on the room. An Indian in a maroon jacket brought in a white cloth and headed for the banqueting table in the centre of the room. Another followed, pushing a squeaking trolley laden with plates of egg sandwiches, cold kebabs, cocktail beef sausages on sticks, miniature doughnuts, rock buns and cheese straws. A third bore a tray of cups, jugs of milk and bowls of sugar and a fourth carried a large pot of tea and a heatproof mat. Bringing up the rear were two young Baluchi boys in Khajali dress, one carrying a bowl of dates and the other with a steaming Arabian coffee-pot in one hand and a nest of little handleless cups in the other.

The cloth was spread and the table was laid. Two of the waiters wheeled the trolley out. The others, including the Baluchi boys, stood by expectantly.

A gecko scuttled up the wall from behind one of the sofas and took up position on a curtain pelmet, from where it contemplated the scene with large, unblinking eyes.

Samir Touqan was looking out of the window.

"Aha... The boss is just leaving... so in short time Miqbil and Co. will be arriving *in sha' Allah*," he announced.

"Oh my God! And *in short time* we'll have to start eating some of this disgusting-looking food," Tulip whispered to Violet with a giggle.

Conversation revived.

"So how are you?" Majid inquired of Rashid, for the third or fourth time.

"May Allah be praised," Rashid replied, for the third or fourth time. "What's your news?"

"Good, may your life be long," said Majid. "How is your health?"

"It's fine, may Allah keep you safe," said Rashid.

The typists discussed Indian and Western recipes gleaned from the *Khajal Times* cookery page and talked about their expatriate relatives in Canada, Australia and the UK, all of whom - they informed each other - were earning astronomical salaries.

The rest engaged in self-conscious small talk about how they spent their spare time and what they felt about living in Khajal.

* * * *

A rumbling of voices was heard outside and the doors opened again to admit Migbil al Ameri, the Personnel Manager, Mubarak al Mansuri, the Head of Development and Training, and an elderly sombre-looking European in a grey suit.

Migbil had moved rapidly up the ladder since nationalisation and he had been in his present post for about four months. Mubarak had also been promoted recently and he was happy in his new job; for the first time in his short career (he was 26 years old) he was finding himself - to his surprise - being paid to do something he actually enjoyed.

"Hello everybody. Thanks for coming," Migbil said, taking a seat beside the guest of honour. "Edward... Good to see you again. I'm sorry we're going to lose you. Or perhaps you're not really going after all? This is getting to be a bit of a habit with you, isn't it?"

"Oh come off it. That's not quite fair," Edward laughed (though not wholeheartedly; the thought of his imminent goodbye speech was nagging at him like a toothache). "I've only tried to escape from you once before and that was in the autumn of 1975."

"As long ago as that? *Wallah*, that's hard to believe. It seems like only yesterday... I don't think you've met Doug Harris, my deputy, have you?" The elderly European extended a bony hand.

"No, we haven't met. How do you do? How do you like Khajal, Mr. Harris?" Edward asked.

"Wonderrful place. Wonderrful," Harris said in a sepulchral tone with an expression on his face suggesting he had recently suffered a bereavement. "Forr me Cadgel is a truly life-enhancing place."

A lugubrious Glaswegian on the verge of retirement, like many of the senior Western expatriates in KNPC he was a square peg in a round hole on contract from Mottled Oil in London. Previously, he had been a manager in their head office's accounts department and his experience and skill in dealing with personnel of any nationality was next to zero.

*　　*　　*　　*

Coffee, dates, snacks and tea were served, eaten and drunk, and Migbil rose to his feet.

"I think I'll do the talking as Edward and I are old friends," he said to Harris. "Unless you'd like to."

"No, I'm sure you would do it better than me," said Harris. The ghost of a smile flickered across his face for a second and a half and faded.

"OK... Well... Good afternoon everyone... Hello again to all of you... I'm not going to take up much of your time as I expect you all want to go home as soon as possible, but I would like to say from my heart that we are going to miss Edward. He has been with us on and off - is that the right expression? - for about eight years... He tried to leave us for Beirut back in 1975 but... well, you know what happened in Lebanon in the mid-1970s. This time he is being sent to Tehran which looks a lot safer... I expect he will tell you more about it in a moment.

"And by the way, most of you may not know this but Edward is probably the only person in history to receive two farewell gifts from this department. Though of course we are not the same company today as we were in 1975. Then we were Mottled Oil and now we're KNPC. And Edward himself is also working for a different company now. In 1975 he was employed by Monotone and now he's employed by Gullible."

"Ahem... Global," Edward said in an undertone.

"Sorry. Global."

He handed Edward a small package. Edward received it with appropriate words of gratitude and opened it. As he expected, it contained a gold-plated pen and pencil set (the same as on the previous farewell occasion). And as was expected of him, he reacted with a fairly convincing show of surprise and delight and passed it round so that it could be admired and praised by all (apart from the Indian waiters and the Baluchi boys, who remained at their posts but smiled to show that they too thought it was a happy occasion).

Now it was Edward's turn to speak.

"Thank you all very much for your generosity," he said. "Just in case any of you think I am pretending to leave so that I can get a free pen and pencil set, let me assure you that this time I really am going... In many ways I am genuinely sad to leave. I've spent almost a quarter of my life in Khajal, some of my best friends are here and I can sincerely say that I regard this country as my second home. And I don't feel that I'm saying good-bye to you for ever, never to return. Iran is only on the other side of the Gulf and I plan to come back here for visits whenever I can.

"I'm looking forward to Tehran. I lived there for a time years ago. In fact it was my first experience of the Middle East... And as Migbil has just said, it is not going to blow up like Beirut did just before I was due to fly there. Of course there have been a few minor disturbances in one or two places in Iran recently... but they can happen in any country and I'm quite confident they won't amount to anything... When Jimmy Carter - you know, the President of the United States... when Carter was a guest of the Shah in Tehran last year he described the country as 'an island of stability in one of the most troubled areas of the world' ... And if that's what he thinks, then who am I to doubt the words of a US President?

"Anyway, many thanks again... And my sincere good wishes to you all. I won't say goodbye, but *au revoir* as I'm sure we will meet again."

After the party Edward accepted Rashid al Khater's offer of a lift back into town.

"I know you told us you were scared but I thought that was quite a good speech you gave," Rashid said as they whizzed along the new dual carriageway between KNPC and Khajal City at ninety miles an hour.

"Thank you. In the end it didn't feel too bad... once I'd got started. And I thought it was a nice, easy atmosphere thanks to Migbil. I've always liked him... It's great to see that you Khajalis are now calling the shots."

"Calling the shots?"

"In control of your own affairs."

"Yes. I know what it means but is that what you seriously think?"

"Yes of course. Don't you? Today the Managing Director is a Khajali, the heads of the departments are all Khajalis and the expatriates are just their assistants. I remember when Migbil was a filing clerk... In fact when I first started working at Mottled Oil he wasn't even that and now he is the Personnel Manager. And I think Mubarak was just an office messenger. But look at him now."

"That's what it might look like from the outside if you don't know what's really happening," Rashid said. "But the truth is rather different. We Khajalis certainly want to take control of our own affairs and it's true that the oil revenues come directly to us these days, not through Mottled Oil... But our Khajali managers are really just pictures on walls."

"What do you mean?"

"The people who make the real decisions are still the so-called assistants - the English. The Khajali bosses - the nominal bosses - have the grand offices and important job titles but it wouldn't actually make any difference if they never came to work at all... Look at Sheikh Hammad bin Ali, our Managing Director - at least that's what they call him. He never arrives at his office before eleven or half past eleven and you only see him after lunch if something really important is happening, like an official visit by a high-up foreign dignitary. Sometimes he never turns up at all if he's got a busy social calendar. The man with the real power is Eric Rodwell, who is officially his deputy... It's the same in all the other departments."

"Even with people like Migbil and Mubarak?"

"Yes. Even people like Migbil and Mubarak, though at least they take their jobs seriously. Their main problem is that they haven't got much experience."

"Is this your personal opinion or do most Khajalis think like you?"

"All Khajalis think like me... including the Emir I imagine. I'm talking about facts, not opinions."

"If that's the case, someone needs to do something about it."

"Don't worry, Edward. We will. We will... Some of us are seriously unhappy about the situation. If we felt Mottled Oil cared about Khajal even slightly we probably wouldn't mind so much, but now that they are receiving a fixed administration fee instead of the profits they are treating KNPC as a rubbish dump. As I understand it, they know that they'll be getting the same amount of money from us whether we operate at a profit or a loss, so they are sending us all their rubbish people that they want to get rid of.

I don't think any of the so-called management they've sent us since nationalisation have been any good."

"Well, I can say one thing," Edward said. "If other Khajalis of your generation are as aware of what's going on as you are, I don't think Khajal needs to worry too much about its long term future. I wish you the best of luck. I mean it."

In the end Edward never made it to Tehran. He and Jimmy Carter (and most of the Western intelligence services) had misread the situation in Iran and by late 1978 the more perceptive observers were beginning to realise that revolution was in the air and the fall of the Shah's regime was a distinct possibility. Chaos was taking over in the major cities, including the capital, and within a week of Edward's Farewell Tea Party No. 2 Global Schools had wisely decided to close down their Iranian operation.

Luckily for him, they had not yet signed up a replacement teacher for him at KNPC, so he was able to stay on in his old job. This time, however, he himself felt ready to move on; middle age was now visible on the horizon and the groundhog day effect of his latest failure to leave for pastures new persuaded him that it was time to stop drifting aimlessly through life.

A few months later he packed his bags for the last time and returned to England to see what the future looked like from there. Within a year he was married to an enterprising young Anglo-Iranian woman he had met through mutual friends, and with her brains and connections and his savings from his years in Khajal they set up a small business importing rustic handicrafts from Iran, Afghanistan, Central Asia and Northern Pakistan for the UK market.

It flourished, and over the next few decades they led a peaceful but adventurous life, based in England but making frequent trips to some of the wilder and more exotic parts of the world to buy new stock. Whenever the opportunity arose, Edward would make a stopover in Khajal to visit his old friends and share their memories of the joys and tribulations of their younger days.

11.

KHAJAL REVISITED

By Edward's son, Matthew

November 2018 - England

Until earlier this year I never knew that my father had written a book. I discovered it a few months ago after he and my mother decided to downsize from their rambling old country house to a bungalow on the edge of Ipswich and asked me to help clear out nearly forty years of accumulated junk.

As I was going through the contents of the old Irish bog-oak escritoire on their upstairs landing, I came across a bundle of dog-eared pages covered with his familiar scrawl.

"Were you planning to do anything with this, Dad?" I asked him after I had had a browse through it.

"That? Hang on... Good God! I didn't realise it was still around. It's the draft of something I was trying to write after I came back from the Gulf in the late seventies. A sort of novel. I thought I'd chucked it out ages ago. We might as well bin it now."

"Certainly not! It's definitely worth keeping... Although it's written in the third person it really looks more like a personal memoir than a novel and... I'm not joking! I think it could be a useful historical record. I'm familiar with the episodes you describe; you've told me about them on and off over the years when you've been in nostalgia mode. Usually prefaced with the words: 'Stop me if you've heard this one before.'"

"Hmm. Yes. It's true that the events I wrote about actually took place. Well, ninety per cent of them anyway. Even the details are mainly correct but I've juggled around with the people they happened to and the sequence and locations in which they occurred. And I've changed the names apart from my own... Funny that it's resurfaced now after all these years. I think the last time I saw it was when I showed it to your Uncle Billy just after I had written it. He told me it was rubbish and made one or two other scathing remarks and I thought I had thrown it away."

"Sod Uncle Billy. It's certainly not rubbish," I said. "It's quite an enjoyable read but I think it needs a proper ending. Couldn't you write another chapter or two just to round it off? As it stands it comes to rather an abrupt halt."

"No," he said. "I'm done with it. After Billy's comments I lost interest completely and now it seems so long ago that I don't feel part of it any more. When I was writing it I felt personally engaged... but, as I say, not anymore."

"How about offering it to a publisher as a factual account and scrapping the pseudonyms, including the name of that fictitious country?"

"You mean Khajal?"

"Yes... Do you seriously think the 'Khajalis', as you call them... Do you seriously think the Khajalis would be offended by this book if you gave their country its proper name? After all, you don't say anything positively rude about it or them. And in any case, from your descriptions of the people and places I'm sure anyone who was living in the Gulf region in the 1970s would recognize it instantly as *****. Pseudonym or no pseudonym."

"Generally speaking, I don't expect most ******s would mind what I've written, but I can think of one or two who might misinterpret my intention and accuse me of attacking their country... Anyway, the whole question is academic because I have no intention of proceeding with it."

April 2019 - England

My father's interest in his old novel/memoir has started to perk up again... possibly as a result of my encouragement though I think the main reason is that we are planning a trip to Khajal next month to see some of his old friends. (On his insistence I haven't changed the name of the country!) He says he doesn't feel like putting pen to paper again himself as he hasn't got the energy to write anything more ambitious than an occasional postcard these days, but he would be happy for me to be his amanuensis.

My mother says she doesn't want to come with us. Although her father's family is from that general neck of the woods (i.e. Iran) and she was born in Tehran, she says the Arab world is boring and the Arabians are backward and uncivilized.

"They sit on the floor and eat with their hands... and with my rheumatic knees I wouldn't be able to do that even if I wanted to," she says.

"These days a lot of Khajalis sit on sofas and eat at dining room tables with knives and forks. And I'm sure if you visited a house where they sit on the floor they would be happy to rustle up a chair for you from somewhere," my father told her.

He has kept in regular but infrequent touch with his old friends over the years and still knows what is going on in Khajal, although the last time he actually went there must have been over thirty years ago. (Moreover, he says, even when he lived there in the dim and distant past before I was born, a lot of the old customs, traditions and practices were already starting to change.)

"Anyway, I don't want to go there. The Arabs don't like us Iranians," my mother said.

"But your mother was English so you're not really Iranian... and in any case a lot of Khajalis are actually of Iranian origin."

"Yes, but they're mostly Sunnis from the coastal area. They're much more like Arabs and I have nothing in common with them. They don't even speak proper Persian."

12th May 2019 - Khajal

We arrived in Khajal three days ago and were met at the airport by Salim - my father's former student and probably his oldest friend. He is in his late sixties now and retired from KNPC some years ago after a career in the Company's Finance Department. I don't know why he ended up there, considering that he originally joined Mottled Oil in 1974 as a technical trainee (See Chapter 2). His son Omar, who is in his forties, joined KNPC in the late 1990s and is now head of the Marine Department.

Of my father's other old friends and colleagues, Migbil died around five years ago (heart attack, according to reports). Mubarak left KNPC in the 1980s and eventually became the local agent for a well-known Japanese electronics company. Today he is unbelievably rich, though he wears his wealth lightly and is still what the Khajalis call "*sha'bi*" (unpretentious, sociable and totally unsnobbish).

We had dinner with him at his house yesterday evening. Rashid al Khater lives in 'Ishsha - originally a small town just to the south of Khajal City but now a suburb of the capital. He left KNPC at a fairly young age when the government poached him and put him in charge of the country's new economic planning department. These days he is a minister and a very busy man, but he has fond memories of my father and he has invited us to spend a couple of nights with him and his family this weekend at his beach house by the southern sand dunes.

Khajal today looks nothing like the Khajal of my father's younger days. In the 1970s it was a rather laid-back, intimate sort of place where not everything worked very efficiently. At least, that was the impression I got from the way my father used to describe it. The whole country had a population of about 150,000, most of them Khajalis or Northern Arabs. Today that population has risen to around two and a half million, only just over ten per cent of whom are nationals.

Khajal City itself is now an enormous, sprawling metropolis and, to be honest, not very pleasant apart from the Corniche, which has a five-mile promenade with well-kept lawns and beds of petunias, African marigolds, canna lilies, lantana bushes and other tropical flowers and shrubs. The rest of the city consists mainly of skyscrapers, high-rise office and apartment blocks topped with huge neon signs advertising global brands, five-star hotels, gleaming white government buildings, Western-style supermarkets and department stores, sterile-looking housing estates of identical white or cream-coloured villas, eight-lane dual carriageways and roundabouts with flowerbeds or large sculptures representing the Municipality's vision of Khajali life and culture.

My father tells me the first skyscraper - a fairly modest affair compared with today's monstrosities - was on the point of completion when he left in 1979. (Somewhere at home we have an old visitors' guide in English published by the Ministry of

Information, which includes a photograph of it with the caption "A SKYCRAPPER ON THE SEAFRONT".)

Not every trace of the old Khajal City has been obliterated. There are still a few narrow streets, alleyways, gypsum and coral houses and *barasti* shacks here and there but they look as if they are the intruders and the brash steel, glass and concrete newcomers are the rightful occupants of this soulless place. Some of the poorer expatriate work force live in the town but most are housed in crowded labour camps on the outskirts.

In the rest of this flat little emirate the desert is criss-crossed with multi-lane highways and dotted with factories, pylons, communication towers, roadside service stations and little shops and cafes, so wherever you happen to be, "civilization" is never more than a few hundred yards away. I fear that peace and quiet can no longer be enjoyed in the open air, except possibly deep in the southern sand dunes (which we haven't visited yet).

On the plus side, Khajal today has an excellent public transport system with regular bus services to every part of the country and a new underground railway staffed by efficient Thais and Filipinos who speak good English but - on the whole - no Arabic. You might think this surprising considering that it in is an Arab country, but very few Khajalis use public transport and the majority of the population who do are non-Arabs who are more at home speaking various versions of English.

"People of our generation long for the old days," Salim says. "Of course now we have all the material things we could want - the things we could only dream about when we were poor... money, big houses, fast cars, holidays in Europe and America... but they are outweighed by what we have lost.

"Our younger people see the world differently of course. My twenty-year-old grandson says he can't imagine how we managed to live the way we did. For him the Khajal of today is a paradise on earth; he thinks it is the best country in the world but he doesn't understand what it is like to be part of a genuine community. I don't think he believes me when I tell him that when I used to go to the *souq* in the early 1970s I always knew half the people there - the customers and passers-by as well as the shopkeepers - and that wherever I happened to be in the town I would be sure to bump into a friend, colleague, relative or acquaintance within a minute or two. These days the streets are full of strangers; we don't really know who we are or even where we belong. Most of the population here today don't speak our language or understand our customs and I think a lot of them resent us locals for our wealth."

"I've heard that relationships between family members are changing too," my father said.

"Yes. Very much so, unfortunately. You remember back in the seventies many of the residential quarters were named after particular clans and we usually lived together under the same roof, even after we got married and started having children of our own. And if things began to get too crowded at home and some of us had to move out we always tried to live next door to each other, or as near to each other as possible. Even those of us with houses outside our traditional areas kept in close touch and we'd have a proper family get-together at least once a week. Now I hardly see even my close family from one week to the next, and in the case of my cousins it's often as rarely as one wedding to the next."

"It sounds a bit like England... What about friends?"

"I'm afraid we've got our priorities the wrong way round these days. In the past it was family, then friends, then work. Now it's work, then friends who can be useful to us, then friends we are fond of and like to spend time with, then, lastly, family. I suppose it's inevitable with the pace of modern life, but it's destroying our culture - and even our ability to love and care for each other."

18th May 2019 - Khajal

We are going home tomorrow. This has been an interesting and enjoyable trip and I would like to stay longer, but summer arrived just after we did and the last two or three days have been too hot for comfort. We had a great weekend with Rashid and spent most of the time swimming, fishing or just lazing on the beach. He took us out on his boat - an old wooden dhow which he has converted into a comfortable cabin cruiser - and I caught a couple of garfish. My father hooked a fair-sized grouper, which the locals call a hamour.

I told Rashid I had read about his comments on Khajal's oil industry after my father's second farewell tea party and asked him if he still felt the same way.

"Yes and no," he said. "I still feel strongly that we ought to be more in control of our own affairs, but in a different way. Now I can't help thinking that any shortcomings in that respect today are our fault and nobody else's."

"Do you mean Khajal should insist on having more control of its political or economic affairs?" I asked him.

"Neither. I'm talking about us Khajalis as individuals. In the past we felt our naivety was being exploited by cunning foreigners. Now I'm sorry to say we are becoming parasitic... if we have not become parasites already. Most of us just want to sit back and let the foreigners do the work while we rake in the benefits without contributing anything ourselves."

"Isn't that something the government ought to be tackling?" I asked.

"There's only so much the government can do. We've had a Khajalisation policy in place since the early 1970s... Admittedly, in the early days we only paid lip service to it because the people in charge still had a servile attitude to the old colonial power and our real rulers were the foreign oil companies and British government advisers. However, over the last thirty years and more we have come a long way. When your father was living here the country had a very poor infrastructure, many of the population were illiterate and things were run in a very haphazard way."

"That's true," my father said. "There was no co-ordination between the government departments. I remember - it must have been around 1976 or 77 - the Roads Department were converting that little street between the floral clock roundabout and the Corniche into a dual carriageway while at the same time the electricity department were building a substation right in its path... So for years there was dual carriageway for two hundred yards, then single carriageway, then dual carriageway again for the rest of the way."

"Ah yes... The floral clock roundabout," Rashid said. "I was still in my teens when they installed the speaking clock in the middle of it. For about a week it shouted out the time in Arabic, every hour on the hour, day and night, then the local stray dogs decided they liked it and made their home in the middle of the dial and blocked up the works. After that it never worked again."

"Anyway, what about Khajalisation now?" I asked.

"Our work force today is probably among the best educated in the world. We've got more PhDs per head of population than anywhere - many with degrees from Western universities. We have scientists, doctors, engineers, management consultants... and I don't know what, but... this is true in the vast majority of cases... most people want administrative jobs in the government. In the West engineers are prepared to get their hands dirty but not here. A Khajali engineer likes to sit behind a big desk in a large office and issue orders. Doctors in other countries accept long and unsociable hours as a condition of the job, but not here..."

"I remember the taboo on tribal people doing certain jobs. Has that got something to do with it?" my father asked.

"That's part of it but not the whole story. Even in the old days when we were poor - or relatively poor - the oil companies were more or less the only places where you would find a Khajali mechanic or tugman. Even tribal people made an exception for manual jobs in the oil industry and believed it was OK if you were employed by Mottled Oil. The other problem is that government jobs have status while private sector jobs - particularly jobs involving manual work - don't. And as for unskilled manual jobs, forget it. A few months ago there was an outcry because the Khajal Palace Hotel advertised for waiters and announced that preference would be given to Khajali applicants... People wrote to the papers and demanded that the Egyptian recruitment manager should be sacked for insulting the population of Khajal."

"Insulting the population of Khajal?"

"Yes. For daring to suggest that a Khajali should do such a menial job."

19th May 2019 - Khajal

We've been in the airport departure lounge for the past three hours because our flight has been delayed due to "a small technical problem", according to the information desk. We should be boarding shortly.

Our visit to this country has been a success on the whole. For me it was a new experience as I have never been to this part of the world before. For my father, even though he knew what to expect it has been in some ways a bit of a shock.

"When I last came here in the late 1980s the country was changing fast... that's true... but at least it was recognizable and none of the major landmarks of the 1970s had disappeared," he said. "The city centre still looked much the same as ever. It had most of the same shops and restaurants that I used to go to...

Shady's... that was the bakery where we used to buy Western-style bread... Ali Mohammed's travel agency... the little grocery in Water Department Street that sometimes sold Iranian caviar... What was it called? Shams, I think... The massive Grand Khajal Hotel still dominated the skyline in splendid isolation at the far end of the Corniche... Now the entire centre of Khajal City has been demolished and rebuilt and I can't relate any of it to what it looked like before. Even the old *souq*, though it still looks like a *souq* but a different *souq*... And you probably didn't even notice the Grand Khajal Hotel. It's still there... I saw it because I was looking out for it, but today it is just a modest little pyramid in the middle of a forest of skyscrapers."

"What are your feelings about the trip then?" I asked.

"I'm pleased that I lived here when I did rather than in... where are we now? ... 2019. I've still got plenty of Khajali friends forty odd years later, but I think that an expatriate coming here today would hardly ever meet a local - except as a passports or customs official at the airport. In the old days we worked together and socialised together, but today - you remember what Mubarak said the other night? These days the Khajalis keep very much to themselves and have little to do with the expatriates. I suppose it's because they are such a tiny minority in their own country now... Just a minute... I think they are calling our flight."

He was right. We are about to head for the boarding gate. We should be back in Ipswich by dinner time this evening.

EPILOGUE

I n 2020 several of the familiar Mottled Oil/KNPC faces from the 1970s were still around, though most of the older ones had died (mainly of natural causes, though at least two of the technical trainees from that era had not - one having drowned on a weekend fishing trip and the other meeting an untimely end in a fire on an offshore oil rig). Of Edward's old trainees who were still alive, the youngest were in their early sixties.

As for the others...

Freddy and Lucinda split up shortly after Freddy's ignominious flight to Paris. He subsequently re-emerged phoenix-like from the ashes of Monotone as an organizer of international language school exhibitions in the capitals of Western Europe, and for the first time in his life he became a genuine, if minor, business tycoon - a role he enjoyed enormously. After the fall of the Soviet Union he branched out into Eastern Europe and when he died in 2004 his son Rupert inherited a large and thriving empire. In the early 1980s Lucinda married a Canadian Sufi and embraced Islam. She and her husband currently provide spiritual guidance to a small Muslim community in the Scottish Highlands.

Of the old Mottled Oil teachers, Mike Kelly made as good a recovery from his car accident as could be hoped. In 1982 he married his long-time girlfriend and the following year they opened a camera shop in Basingstoke which continues as a well-established family business to this day. He retired a few years ago and since then it has been managed by his daughter and her husband, though he still takes an active interest in it and works there one day a week "just to keep my hand in".

After a year at KNPC with Global Schools, Dick left Khajal to become a tourist guide taking small groups on trips round France, Germany, Switzerland and Italy. A rolling stone and fluent in French and German, his sociable nature was well suited to life on the road but two years into the job he suffered a massive stroke one night in his hotel room on the shores of Lake Geneva and was found dead in his bed the following morning.

Roy Sladen left Khajal after a year with Global and enrolled at Essex University as a mature linguistics student. By the mid-1980s he was a senior lecturer at a university in the Midlands, where he stayed until he retired in 2010. He and his wife Helen now live in Brittany.

Steve Kettle stayed on in Khajal for the rest of his working life. In 1982 he left Global's employ and joined KNPC as a training officer (which in practice meant that he carried on in his old job as an English teacher). Over the following years he rose slowly up the career ladder and by the time he retired in the early 2000s he gloried in the grand(ish) title of Deputy Chief Training Superintendent - as assistant and adviser to a young Khajali who had recently returned from the United States with a doctorate in business management. He now lives in Turkey.

Peter Frazer's relationship with Global was never harmonious, though when he left them it was his decision, not theirs, mainly because he was a competent teacher and quite popular with his trainees as well as KNPC's Khajali management. After his departure in 1983 he went to Pakistan on an impulse and ended up in the Swat Valley as manager of a new hotel in Mingora that had ambitions to feature in the British Sunday colour supplements. (The owner - a relative of the last Akhund of Swat - was an Old Harrovian with fond memories of his years in England.) Somewhat to its proprietor's chagrin, the hotel never became a household name in international circles but it gained a reputation among Western visitors as a pleasantly quirky establishment that offered some of the comforts of home. (To his surprise, Peter discovered that he had hidden talents as a cook and interior decorator and his cheese soufflés and Lancashire hot pots were warmly praised in travellers' tales from Berlin to San Francisco. The elegant style of the bedrooms, too, received favourable comment in a couple of French and Spanish backpackers' guidebooks.)

He fled to Karachi after the Pakistani Taliban seized control of Swat during the first decade of the 21st century, though he later returned to Mingora when peace was restored and today he is still living in the Swat Valley.

George Weever retired shortly after Mottled Oil was nationalised and he and his wife Dorothy returned to their cottage in the English home counties, where their lives followed the conventional Old Mottledite pattern (golf club, gardening, local charities and meals out at olde worlde pubs). He died in 2005 at the age of 85.

Hussain Abbas al Marri continued in his mainly ceremonial role as KNPC Chairman until the turn of the millennium, when the Ruler decided it was time to give someone else a go. For his remaining years (by then he was in his late sixties) he devoted his energies to his highly lucrative construction company - a business he had started when he was still a humble clerk at Mottled Oil over thirty years earlier. He died in 2009.

Kamal survived the changes after Mottled Oil became KNPC, though his new Khajali boss made sure that his hands were kept a safe distance away from the levers of power. He retired in 1998 and bought a small novelty and gift shop in Khajal City. As a Palestinian refugee he had a permanent right of residence in the country and in 2002 he finally achieved his long-cherished ambition of becoming a Khajali citizen.

"But he's still a Palestinian," Salim said. "He'll never be one of us."

"I never think of him as being really one of us," Samir Touqan said. "We Palestinians don't trust him any more than the Khajalis do."

www.ingramcontent.com/pod-product-compliance
Ingram Content Group UK Ltd.
Pitfield, Milton Keynes, MK11 3LW, UK
UKHW041847070725
460516UK00004B/9